# "The Boy."

Ice clinked against an heirloom crystal glass as he took it from a wrought-iron table. Draining it, he poured another drink from a decanter he'd brought into the garden with him.

*The boy.* It was always that, never more. The child's name was Cade. Yet for reasons he wouldn't define, Lincoln Cade couldn't bring himself to call Linsey's son by his own name.

"Who is he, Linsey? Why is his hair dark like mine? Who gave him my name?"

Laughter from the street intruded. Adult amusement, but in it Lincoln heard the haunting laugh of a child.

But whose child?

Turning to the house, forsaking the garden and his search for peace he knew would elude him for a long time to come, Lincoln knew what he must do. He knew what he would do.

For Linsey, for himself.

For the boy.

Dear Reader,

Welcome to the world of Silhouette Desire, where you can indulge yourself every month with romances that can only be described as passionate, powerful and provocative!

Fabulous BJ James brings you June's MAN OF THE MONTH with *A Lady for Lincoln Cade*. In promising to take care of an ex-flame—and the widow of his estranged friend—Lincoln Cade discovers she has a child. Bestselling author Leanne Banks offers another title in her MILLION DOLLAR MEN miniseries with *The Millionaire's Secret Wish*. When a former childhood sweetheart gets amnesia, a wealthy executive sees his chance to woo her back.

Desire is thrilled to present another exciting miniseries about the scandalous Fortune family with FORTUNES OF TEXAS: THE LOST HEIRS. Anne Marie Winston launches the series with *A Most Desirable M.D.*, in which a doctor and nurse share a night of passion that leads to marriage! Dixie Browning offers a compelling story about a sophisticated businessman who falls in love with a plain, plump woman while stranded on a small island in *More to Love*. Cathleen Galitz's *Wyoming Cinderella* features a young woman whose life is transformed when she becomes nanny to the children of her brooding, rich neighbor. And Kathie DeNosky offers her hero a surprise when he discovers a one-night stand leads to pregnancy and true love in *His Baby Surprise*.

Indulge yourself with all six Desire titles—and see details inside about our exciting new contest, "Silhouette Makes You a Star."

Enjoy!

*Joan Marlow Golan*

Joan Marlow Golan
Senior Editor, Silhouette Desire

Please address questions and book requests to:
Silhouette Reader Service
U.S.: 3010 Walden Ave., P.O. Box 1325, Buffalo, NY 14269
Canadian: P.O. Box 609, Fort Erie, Ont. L2A 5X3

# A Lady for Lincoln Cade
## BJ JAMES

Published by Silhouette Books

**America's Publisher of Contemporary Romance**

For Gay, a friend, a lady.

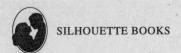 SILHOUETTE BOOKS

ISBN 0-373-76369-7

A LADY FOR LINCOLN CADE

Copyright © 2001 by BJ James

This edition published by arrangement with Harlequin Books S.A.

® and TM are trademarks of Harlequin Books S.A., used under license. Trademarks indicated with ® are registered in the United States Patent and Trademark Office, the Canadian Trade Marks Office and in other countries.

Visit Silhouette at www.eHarlequin.com

**Printed in U.S.A.**

## BJ JAMES'

first book for Silhouette Desire was published in February 1987. Her second Desire title garnered for BJ a second Maggie, the coveted award of Georgia Romance Writers. Through the years there have been other awards and nominations for awards, including, from *Romantic Times Magazine,* Reviewer's Choice, Career Achievement, Best Desire and Best Series Romance of the Year. In that time, her books have appeared regularly on a number of bestseller lists, among them Waldenbooks and *USA Today.*

On a personal note, BJ and her physician husband have three sons and two grandsons. While her address reads Mooreboro, this is only the origin of a mail route passing through the countryside. A small village set in the foothills of western North Carolina is her home.

# FOREWORD

In the coastal Lowcountry of South Carolina where the fresh waters of winding rivers flow into the sea, there is an Eden of unmatched wonders. In this mix of waters and along the shores by which they carve their paths, life is rich and varied. The land is one of uncommon contrasts with sandy, seaswept beaches, mysterious swamps, teeming marshes bounded by ancient maritime forests. And the multitude of creatures that abide in each.

In this realm of palms, and palmettos, estuaries and rivers, shaded by towering live oaks draped in ghostly Spanish moss, lies Belle Terre. Like an exquisite pearl set among emeralds and sapphires, with its name the small antebellum city describes its province. As it describes itself.

*Belle Terre, beautiful land.* A beautiful city.

A very proper, very elegant, beautiful city. A gift for the soul. An exquisite mélange for the senses. With ancient and grand structures in varying states of repair and disrepair set along tree-lined, cobbled streets. With narrow, gated gardens lush with such greenery as resurrection and cinnamon ferns. And all of it wrapped in the lingering scent of camellias, azaleas, jasmin, and magnolias.

Steeped in an aura of history, its culture and customs influenced by plantations that once abounded in the Lowcountry, as it clings to its past Belle Terre is a province of contradictions. Within its society one will find arrogance abiding with humility, cruelty with kindness, insolence with gentility, honor with depravity, and hatred with love.

As ever when the senses are whetted and emotions untamed, in Belle Terre there will be passion, romance, and scandal.

# One

"Linc! Ho, Lincoln."

Long after the call faded, the pounding of a horse's hooves sheared through the stillness settling over the west pasture of Belle Reve. Sighing for the calm of a lost moment, weary after another of too many days routinely beginning with his veterinary practice and ending with duties at his family's historic plantation, Lincoln Cade wearily abandoned his inspection of a sagging fence. From the shade of his battered Stetson he stared into the canted light of the sun falling over lush, sprawling fields common in South Carolina's lowcountry.

Horse and rider were only a dark shape galloping over rich grass. Concerned that this was more than Jesse Lee's usual attack on life, Lincoln stepped forward, catching the horse's bridle as it halted. Instinctively calming the spirited animal, he demanded, "What's wrong, Jesse? Is it Gus?"

"No, boy. Ain't nothing wrong with your dad," the

cowboy explained. "Nothing a mood-sweetening elixir wouldn't fix."

Lincoln laughed. "How many times has he fired you today?"

"A dozen." The laconic answer accompanied a wry grin.

"How many times have you threatened to vamoose, leaving South Carolina in the dust on your way back to Arizona?"

Jesse Lee's mouth widened, rippling the mass of wrinkles scoring his weathered face. "'Bout the same, I reckon."

"If it isn't Gus, then why the hurry?"

Slapping a pocket, Jesse drew out a packet he handed to Lincoln. "The postmaster in Belle Terre sent this special 'cause it was marked urgent by a postmaster in Oregon. I figgered it could wait till you came to the house for supper. But Miz Corey said not. And when Miz Corey says git, any man in his right mind gits.

"When he hired the lady to keep house at Belle Reve, I doubt Gus counted on getting a ramrod for the plantation and him, too. Anyway, she said pronto, and I hightailed it down here."

The wrangler's look strayed to the packet. Lincoln didn't notice. He was hardly aware of anything but the postmark.

"Seems odd, don't it?"

As the horse nuzzled at his shoulder, Jesse's comment penetrated Lincoln's distraction. "Odd?" he asked. "Why?"

"I dunno." Jesse grumbled. "Just strikes me as peculiar coming from an Oregon postmaster. Hope it ain't bad news. Bad news is terrible enough. Gittin' it by mail is worse."

Lincoln gripped the packet. "You think it's bad?"

Jesse's bleak look met Lincoln's. "I don't know who you know in Oregon, but I got a feelin'. The minute Miz

Corey handed it to me, I felt the chill of it skittering down my spine.''

*Oregon.* Lincoln hadn't thought of Oregon in a long time. He hadn't let himself think of it. Until now.

He tried for a smile, remembering the old cowboy was obsessively superstitious. An obsession that went beyond black cats and ladders, and had nothing to do with the grief settling in his own chest. ''I don't feel anything, Jesse,'' he lied. ''So maybe everything's all right.''

''There's one way to find out.'' The older man waited in a mix of worry and curiosity. ''Ain't you gonna open it?''

''When I'm done here.'' Sliding the packet into his back pocket, wondering if Jesse's dire prediction prompted a reluctance to open it in his presence, Lincoln took up the hammer he'd yet to use. ''I'll read it then.''

''In other words, good news or bad, you'll read it alone.''

''Yes,'' Lincoln admitted. ''Good news or bad. And whoever.''

''Tarnation, why didn't you say so?'' Wheeling the horse around, Jesse set his hat more securely. ''Ain't none of this my business. Anyway, who do I know in Oregon?''

''I don't know, Jesse,'' Lincoln said mildly. ''Who do you know in Oregon?''

Tapping the horse's flank, Jesse set it into a run. Nearly lost in hoofbeats, one word drifted back, ''Nobody.''

Horse and rider were beyond sight when Lincoln laid the hammer aside again and took the mail from his pocket. Head down, face shaded by the brim of his hat, he stared at the official cachet. Then, catching a breath, he broke the seal.

A form letter with an added hand-printed message, then two small envelopes banded with red string tumbled into his hand. Reining in clamoring concern, laying the banded letters on a fence post, Lincoln attended the official letter first.

"Dear Mr. Cade," he read aloud, his gaze racing over the paper. "As acting postmaster, I offer my apologies for the delayed delivery of these letters. Due to the ill health of the former postmaster, unfortunately some pieces of mail were put aside and never processed. Among them, these bearing your address. I sincerely hope the delay causes no difficulties. Please be confident steps have been taken to assure..."

Lincoln stared at the envelopes with the absurd bit of string catching the light, gleaming against the creamy squares like a rivulet of scarlet. Bearing the postmark of the same tiny Oregon village, but two weeks apart, one was addressed in the scrawl of a man he'd known all his life, the second in the less familiar hand of a woman. A woman, despite the lies he told himself, he hadn't forgotten in six long years.

Folding the apologetic form, he tucked it away before retrieving the mysterious lost letters. Untying the band of scarlet, letting it drift to the ground, he weighed his choices.

His hands were shaking as he traced the feminine script of one, but steadied again as he shuffled it aside. His decision was made—he would read them in the order of their postmarks.

With an ache in his heart, he lifted the flap of the first envelope and took out a single sheet of paper. When it was finished, he read the second as he had the first—slowly, his lips a sad, grim line. When he was done, his gaze lifted to the horizon, not seeing the sky in its shifting moods.

Time crept by with little variation in the long summer day. Yet for Lincoln it seemed to fly, too fast, too irrevocably. As life had with its changes, leaving things unsettled and things undone. Until it was too late.

Rousing, he gathered his tools, wrapped them, and tied them behind his saddle. The fence could wait. Tugging his horse's reins from a nearby shrub, he stepped into the saddle. Out of habit the horse turned toward home. Toward

Belle Reve. "Not yet, Diablo," Lincoln muttered. "We have a stop to make first."

Setting the stallion into a canter, he guided the massive animal over the pasture fence and onto a little-used path. Then, giving Diablo his head, trusting the old horse to recognize the land and remember the way to their destination, Lincoln let his mind wander to times past...and friends lost.

The passage from the west pasture of Belle Reve to the end of his journey was not long. But when horse and rider emerged from the wooded trail into a clearing, the sun had dipped below the trees, spangling leaves and limbs with dusty gold. This was Stuart land. The bane of land-hungry Cades, a haven for others.

With an eye for beauty and convenience, the first Stuart had set the farmhouse at the edge of a clearing by a narrow creek. A creek that marked Stuart-Cade boundaries as it meandered to the river and finally the sea.

Once there was hardly a day that Lincoln hadn't spent a stolen hour or two in this forbidden place. Now, drawing Diablo to a halt as he surveyed the grounds bathed in the splendor of sunset, he realized years had passed since he'd sought its refuge.

Beyond a crop of weeds threading through volunteer flowers, herbs and vegetables still thriving in rich soil, the farm hadn't changed. If one didn't count the absence of life and laughter a change, he thought somberly, while dismounting by the steps. As he climbed the stairs, a rotting board broke beneath his weight, shattering the myth, reminding Lincoln that more than six years had passed since Frannie Stuart lived and died here. More than six years since she'd filled the house with love and laughter.

How many times had he raced across the west field as a boy, hurrying from a cold, forbidding plantation to the warmth and love that abounded in this small farm? How often had he envied his best friend the wonderful lady who was his mother?

But just as Frannie Stuart always had a hug for any of the Cade boys, and especially Lincoln, Lucky never resented it. With a heart as big and warm as his mother's, Leland Stuart, christened Lucky by his friends, gladly and unselfishly shared.

Boot heels clattering in the silence, Lincoln climbed the rest of the stairs and crossed the porch. When he tried the door, it opened. Not surprising, for he couldn't recall a time it had ever been locked. Ducking beneath the door frame, he stepped inside, into memories of the boy who had stood where a man stood now. Memories so vivid he could hear Lucky's cry of welcome and smell Frannie's cookies baking. Cookies meant to be snitched by hungry boys who had slipped away from chores to fish or hunt and play Tarzan in the swamp.

Drawing himself to his full height, Lincoln looked around him. There were cobwebs and dust everywhere. The musty scent of neglect mingled with a lingering hint of flowers. But nothing had been touched. Frannie and Lucky could have just stepped out intending to return, yet never had.

Wandering through the house, Lincoln paused at the door of the smallest bedroom. The trophies Lucky won in baseball still lined a single shelf. One of his own was there. So was a lure he'd made, and a photo taken when both he and Diablo were young. As if blinders fell from his eyes, Lincoln realized how much a part he'd been allowed to play, *welcomed* to play, in the Stuart home.

Lucky had no father, nor any recollection of ever having one. Lincoln had no mother. Perhaps that had first drawn them to each other. But the bond of affection and shared interests that made them friends and blood brothers, was much stronger.

From grade school, through Belle Terre Academy and the university, he and Lucky had been inseparable. Evidence of their friendship still lived in a simple farmhouse on a rich piece of land lying between a creek and the plantation called Belle Reve.

Like the Cades, the Stuarts were an old family, prominent in South Carolina's lowcountry. And like the Cades, their early wealth had long been lost. By the time Frannie made her debut, little more than respect filled the Stuart coffers. They were an aging but cordial and modern-thinking people. She was their adventurous darling with places to go and things to do. Frannie was a few months past forty, with her daring adventures behind her, when she returned to Belle Terre with Lucky, a babe in arms.

Undaunted by the scandal of bearing an illegitimate child, she settled on the farm, living quietly, meagerly, as was apparent in her bedroom, which Lincoln realized now was pitifully lacking in the feminine pleasures that would have become her. Frannie might have been reduced to creating her own unforgettable fragrance of wild roses and dried flowers, but her capacity for love, her courageous sense of adventure, never faltered.

It was, instead, bequeathed to Lucky. And, as he stared at a photo, encased in a tarnished silver frame, Lincoln realized both had been Frannie's ultimate gift to him, as well.

Caught up in recollections of two wide-eyed boys sitting before a fire, listening to stories of where she'd been and what she'd done, Lincoln continued his sentimental passage. As he came full circle, his lips tilted in a poignant smile for old memories and old friendships that could never be again.

When he returned to the porch, the last rays of the sun had painted the sky a deep vermilion, seeming to set the world ablaze. Lincoln hadn't meant to stay, but, wrapped in light so familiar, he found himself drawn to the steps.

To sit where he'd sat with Lucky. To remember the dreams they'd dreamed on days like this. The days when they were so sure they would live forever and be friends forever and share every great adventure the world had to offer.

"Every great adventure, planned right here." Lincoln looked at the photograph still clutched in his hand. "Even the last, the one that would destroy our friendship as we knew it."

Wearily Lincoln stood. Making note of the step in need of repair, he crossed the overgrown yard to Diablo. Speaking quietly to the grazing horse, he mounted. Hesitating, he watched as light warming the walls of the house faded and darkened, leaving it in shadows. A lonely derelict, waiting.

"For what?" Lincoln wondered aloud. But he didn't need to wonder. He knew.

"For want of love and laughter, a home becomes a house," he whispered, quoting his beloved Frannie. "For want of life, a house becomes a hovel."

Frannie Stuart had been dead nearly seven years. Lucky, for three months. He couldn't change the past, but as he turned Diablo from the Stuart farm, Lincoln vowed that no matter how long it took, he would repay a debt incurred six years before.

A debt called in today, by a letter from the grave.

"Let's go home, Diablo," Lincoln murmured hoarsely. "I have work to do, a lady to find, and promises to keep."

# Two

"Special delivery." Basket in hand, Haley Garrett stood in the open doorway, waiting for Lincoln to abandon his intense study of the evening sky. As she'd spoken, his shoulders tensed. When he turned, a pallor lay over his sundarkened face.

"Lincoln?" Alarm threaded through Haley's voice. "Is something wrong? You look like you've seen a ghost."

Blinking, clearing his vision, Lincoln denied her concern. "Nothing's wrong. My mind was wandering, I thought…"

"That I was her?" Troubled by his mood, Haley stepped into his office uninvited. "Yes, Lincoln, *her*. Linsey Stuart, the woman for whom you've searched for weeks."

"How do you know about Linsey?"

Setting the basket laden with food on his desk, she smiled ruefully. "It would be hard *not* to know, since your search has been conducted by telephone and our office isn't exactly soundproof."

Lincoln moved to his desk. "I never meant to disturb you."

"You didn't. I haven't said anything before because it was none of my business." Haley tilted her head, negating the great difference in their size as she held his gaze. "As your veterinary partner and friend, I'm making it my business now."

Lincoln grasped a pen, tapping it on his desk. "I haven't held up my end of our agreement?"

Catching his hand, she stopped his drumming. "Just the opposite. You're driving yourself. Take today, for instance. You were called to Petersens' to deliver a breech colt at 3:00 a.m. To Hank's dairy at 6:00 a.m. to deal with a sick cow."

Releasing him, she ticked off more stops. "You admitted skipping breakfast, then lunch. If Miss Corey hadn't worried and sent this basket, I suspect you would skip dinner."

"How does skipping meals affect our partnership, Haley?"

*"Partnership."* Haley emphasized her point. "That's the key word. I could have made some of those calls. Given how hard you've been working, I should have made all of them."

"Today was too much for me," he drawled. "But not you?"

"Yes. Because I'm not consumed by a problem." Taking a tarnished frame from his desk, she asked, "Is this Linsey Stuart?"

Lincoln's gaze turned to the photo plundered from the Stuart farm. Where a step awaited repair. "Linsey, Lucky and me. In Montana, our last year at smoke jumpers annual training."

"Linsey Stuart parachuted into forest fires?" The woman in the photograph was small, with an aura of elegance. Haley could believe an adventurous sportswoman, but not smoke jumping.

"No one believed she could do it then, either." Lincoln's mouth quirked in a melancholy smile at Haley's disbelief. "But she did. We all did. That's where our paths crossed—the first summer of jumper training. Lucky and I had been friends all our lives—the moment we met her, she fit.

"Linsey grew up in an orphanage, we became her family." He glanced at the photo of three figures dressed for a jump, exhilarated by the challenge. "We were a team—Lucky Stuart, Linsey Blair, Lincoln Cade. We were called the Three L's."

"This was taken the last year—was it your last jump?"

Lincoln struggled to ease the constriction in his chest. "After the photograph was taken, Lucky was called home. His mother was ill. Two months later he came back. We jumped one more time."

Haley wondered why only one. Lincoln loved jumping. It was in his voice. Even now. "What happened?"

Lincoln's gaze lifted to Haley. But his mind, and perhaps his heart, had stepped back in time. Memories couldn't be hurried. Keeping the gaze that saw another face, she waited.

"We were in Oregon." His voice was distant, as if it came from the faraway place of his thoughts. "The fire had burned for weeks, with jumpers fighting winds as much as the blaze. We were backing each other, as always, when the current shifted and the fire turned, cutting us off from the rest of the crew."

He fell silent; she waited. Again her wait was rewarded.

"Lucky had a knack for maps—he recalled a river. We ran for it and into a slide. Our radios were broken. A head injury left me confused, unsteady on my feet. I couldn't walk out."

"But Linsey and Lucky did?" Haley dared comment into the staccato retelling of a life-and-death drama.

"Only Lucky." Lincoln turned to the window, seeing wind-fanned flames and falling earth beyond its panes. "The fire turned again, and we stumbled on a shack on secure ground. By then it was clear I'd suffered a concussion at the least. Lucky calculated that with burned ground, the slide, and the river as fire breaks, we had a little time before the blaze circled around. Leaving Linsey to look after me, he walked out alone.''

"Through the fire, Lincoln?"

"Through burned paths that could reignite at any time. If they had—'' Halting, he turned a bleak face to Haley, then away again. "Lucky risked his life for mine.''

"And for Linsey,'' Haley murmured, studying his profile. Seeing heartache he'd hidden from the world.

As her classmate in veterinary studies, he'd revealed nothing personal. He wouldn't now, if he weren't exhausted and hurting. Yet, because she knew Lincoln, she knew there was more. Something left unsaid. Haley went where intuition led. "You loved her.''

"We both did.''

"So you stepped aside.'' When he didn't respond, she asked, "Where is Lucky now?''

"Lucky died.'' He looked away. "Four months ago.''

Haley blinked back tears for a grieving friend, for a stranger called Lucky. For a rare friendship. "I'm sorry.''

"Yeah.'' A hand briefly shielded his eyes. "So am I.''

"And now you're looking for his wife. To help.''

"For Lucky's sake. I wasn't there when he needed me, but I thought…'' He seemed to lose himself in a mood. In a moment he spoke again. "Shortly after he died, Linsey left Oregon and dropped out of sight. With no family and no roots, she could be anywhere. Nobody I've hired has found a trace of her.''

Lincoln said nothing more, and Haley wouldn't question his search for Lucky Stuart's widow. Whatever his reason, it wouldn't be to trade on the past, nor because he loved her still. Lincoln Cade wasn't a man who would barter on grief.

No matter what prompted his search, Haley hoped he

would find Linsey Stuart. If it was right, she hoped they would find love and peace together. But that was for another time, another place. And, she suspected, for reconciled lovers to discover.

"It's late, Lincoln. You're exhausted, and I'm famished. Shall we share this thoughtful repast and call it a day?"

He smiled at her ploy to entice him to eat. But as he accepted the sandwich she offered, Haley saw the laughter left the silver of his eyes untouched.

Lincoln considered the wire and the tuft of brown fur caught on a barb. For the third time in a week he'd checked the deteriorating west pasture fence and the second time he'd found evidence of an animal passing near or through the wire. His first thought was deer. Closer inspection suggested dogs.

Among the mongrels of Belle Reve, some were white, some blond, some black. None were brown.

The west pasture was isolated, bordered by two rivers, the sprawl of Belle Reve, and Stuart land. No inhabited houses or farms were close enough for straying pets or working dogs. That left the threat of a pack of lost or abandoned pets. Dogs that would run a horse to death for the joy of the chase.

The Black Arabian stock his brother Jackson kept in pastures at the plantation were far too valuable to dismiss suspicions of a pack gone wild. He decided he would warn Jackson and enlist his aid in trapping the animals. Catching the pommel of his saddle and stepping into the stirrup, Lincoln mounted Diablo.

His inspection complete, he sat for an indecisive moment, trying to resist the lure of the path beyond the fence. The path that would lead to the Stuart farm. In the end he succumbed to a need he'd battled for weeks.

"Won't hurt to check the property." As Diablo's black ears flicked at the sound of his voice, with his palm Lincoln stroked the stallion's mane. "Could be the pack settled in the barn. And there's a step to measure for repair."

Glancing at the sky, gauging the position of the sun, he tapped the horse with the reins. "A couple of hours of daylight left, Diablo. Time enough."

Diablo was eager to run. Lincoln himself enjoyed the rush as the Arabian topped the fence and raced over the corridor that a century before had been the Stuarts' wagon route to town.

Beyond sight of the farm, Lincoln slowed to a walk. If the dogs had made their den on the property, they would be gone before he could find it, if he came riding in like the Lone Ranger.

"Easy, boy. No sudden moves." He walked the horse slowly, barely rustling the grass that grew knee high. "Don't want to spook them if they're here."

With a grunt hardly stifled, he jerked to a startled halt. "What the devil?"

Bending in the saddle, peering through a copse of massive trees, he saw light. Light where there should be no light, gleaming through windows of the Stuart farmhouse.

Illusion? A trick of the sun glinting off glass? Intruders or looters after all these years of the farmhouse standing unlocked?

Maybe. He could persuade himself to accept that. But the creak of rusty hinges was neither a trick nor an illusion. Nor was the woman who pushed open the door and stepped onto the porch. With her hair gleaming like spilling gold, as she shaded her eyes against the glare of the sun, she was familiar and very real.

"Linsey?" Her name was a raw undertone lost in the prattle of breeze-stirred oaks. Yet, spoken in his own voice, it resounded in his mind. Like a man too long in the dark catching a glimpse of the sun, his gaze moved over her. With incredulous care, he committed to mind a memory, seeking first the differences imposed by time and living.

Then the unchanging qualities six long years couldn't sweep from his mind.

Her hair was still long. Still a mass of curls gathered brutally into a topknot by a clasp that never had a chance of holding it. The hand that pushed tumbling strands from her cheeks was still absently impatient.

Her chin still tilted in eternal determination. While her mouth curved in a smile that seemed joyfully childlike and sensual at once. Lincoln wondered if she still caught her lower lip between her teeth when she concentrated or when she worried.

Drawing himself from the aching study of her mouth and face, he matched this Linsey of flesh and blood to the woman he'd turned away from...for Lucky.

She stood tall, shoulders back, making the most of those few inches by which she topped five feet. And as the breeze that sent tiny oak leaves spiraling around him swept across the clearing, molding her supple shirt against her, Lincoln realized her breasts were rounder, fuller. A girlish innocence had given way to an earthy maturity, a beguiling voluptuousness. A metamorphosis making her jean-clad waist and hips seem slimmer.

He'd lost a girl six years ago. Today, he found a woman in full bloom.

To the rest of the world she'd always been a pretty girl full of life and courage. To Lincoln, she was breathtaking from the first. But not so beautiful as now. Never so beautiful he could hardly believe she was real, not illusion.

Just as he could hardly believe that, after hiring investigators to search all of Oregon, Montana, and as many locales in between as possible, he had found her here. Exactly where she should be, in Lucky Stuart's South Carolina home.

The last place he'd thought to look in a month. The last place he would ever think to look, if the search hadn't ended.

How long had she been here? One week? Two? How soon after his last stop by the farm had she arrived? "How long before you were going to let me know, Linsey?"

As relieved as he was that she was here, like a battering ram striking out of nowhere, Lincoln was filled with anger bordering on rage. Anger laced with bitter self-disgust that any of it should matter. That *she* should matter.

For years he'd struggled to put the past in perspective. From a passionate and desperate interlude in a shack in an Oregon forest surrounded by fire, to the day he walked her down the aisle—giving her, in an unknown father's stead, to Lucky—he thought he'd finally succeeded in putting it behind him.

Until the letters. Then he knew his struggles and all he believed he'd accomplished had been a farce.

Farce or not, his life was on an even keel, he didn't want it disrupted by old wounds torn open. He hadn't stopped to think of this moment when he'd begun the search. He hadn't thought of anything but the wishes of a dying friend. But now, after the month and a small fortune spent searching for her, after the anguish of every minute of each of those days, he was tempted to ride away as if he'd never seen her and never loved her.

Dear God, he was tempted, but he'd never broken a promise to Lucky. He wouldn't now. Raking an arm over his face, wishing he could wipe the anger from his heart as easily as he could from his features, he lifted a hand to hail the house.

"Cade."

Lincoln froze at the sound, hand uplifted, lips parted in a greeting he wouldn't utter.

"Cade? Where are you, tiger? Better come inside before it gets dark."

Shocked that she could know he was there in the shadows that deepened with every increment the sun sank, Lincoln didn't respond. He couldn't respond as her voice flowed over him filled with love, driving out the anger.

In that moment of stunned silence, he heard the bark of a dog, a peal of laughter, then the voice of a child. "I'm here, Mom. In the barn with Brownie."

Before he could make sense of it, a small boy appeared at the barn door. A boy called Cade and his dog.

"Brownie." Lincoln didn't know why it was that name he muttered. He didn't understand why barbwire streaming with brown dog hair twice in three days should flood his mind. But he was glad for a small boy's simple name for a brown dog and for the mystery of the barbs' trophies solved.

Mind candy, a mental dodge. A name and a mystery more easily understood and resolved than the one Lincoln confronted in gathering darkness beyond the clearing of the Stuart farm.

His mouth was dry, his head hurt, his heart pounded so hard he thought it might explode. He didn't want to stay, but he couldn't drag his gaze from the boy as he raced across the yard and skipped over the broken step into his mother's arms.

He was a small boy, but too big for Linsey to pick up. Yet she did, crushing him to her as she spun him round and round, planting nibbling kisses on his neck. The boy's laughter escalated to squeals and giggles, while the dog jumped in circles, trying to join in.

Breathless and panting, Linsey stopped spinning. When she was still again, Lincoln watched as the boy plucked the clasp from her hair, letting it fall beyond her shoulders.

Catching a strand in his grubby fist, he laughed in delight. "Pretty."

Linsey laughed, too. "Ah, shucks, kind sir. I bet you say that to all the girls."

"Nope." The boy giggled and squirmed, and giggled that much harder when she tickled him. "Just you."

"That will change in a few years." Linsey's laugh faded as she hugged him again. "You like it here, don't you, Cade?"

"Yep." The boy's head bobbed. "But I was wondering."

"Yeah?"

"Can I have a horse?"

"Hmm." Linsey tilted her head, considering. "I suppose one day. What kind of horse would you want?"

"A humongous black one, like the tall man."

In the shadows Lincoln tensed, waiting for Linsey to look into the falling night. The air had grown unnaturally still; every sound carried as if it were magnified. He found himself holding his breath and keeping Diablo under a tight rein as he awaited discovery.

"A tall man with a humongous horse? I don't know who you mean, tiger." The porch lay in shadow now, obscuring Linsey's features. "Is this a character from TV?"

The boy shook his head with the emphatic impatience of the young. "Nope. A real man." A finger pointed. "He was over there."

"He was?" Linsey's chin lifted sharply. Frowning, she concentrated on the area her son indicated. "Do you see him now?"

"Nope. I could see him from the loft, though." The boy, whose hair was as dark as his mother's was fair, gestured again toward the bit of deserted trail visible from the porch.

"You climbed to the loft?" Linsey's smile faltered. Even to a watcher, hovering and hidden, her demeanor changed, though she spoke kindly to the boy. "We discussed that we had to go carefully here. The house and barn are old, they've been empty and neglected for a long time. Do you remember what else I said?"

"There could be rotten boards to fall through, and spiders, and snakes," the boy finished for her. "I remembered, Mom, and I was careful. Real careful."

"Why did you go there?" Linsey wasn't yet pacified.

The boy lifted both shoulders in a vague response. "I dunno, 'cept I just wanted to look. It's pretty, Mom. I could see the river and the trees, and almost to Oregon. But I won't go again, if you don't want me to."

"Promise? Just until I can get around to repairing it?"

Solemnly the boy drew a sweeping cross over his chest and stomach. "Cross my heart."

"Promise accepted." A loving finger tapped his nose, signaling his trespass was forgiven but not forgotten. "What do you say we finish the chocolate pudding left from supper?"

"Can I have my horse, too?"

"The humongous one?"

"Yep."

Linsey hugged him again. "We'll see. Good enough?"

"Yep."

"Can you say anything but yep, tiger?"

"Yep," the boy answered gravely, then dissolved into giggles at the repartee that was obviously a long-standing game.

In a dancing step Linsey took her son to the door. Pausing there, she turned back. For a sinking moment, though he knew she couldn't see into the dark cave of trees, Lincoln could feel her gaze strafing over him.

For too long she stood in the doorway, looking from the treeline to the stream, then toward the end of the trail. But Linsey was new to the area—she wouldn't know this was the passage she'd heard Lincoln call the escape route. She wouldn't know the long-abandoned trail had led a traveler back to the farm again.

Lincoln's tension telegraphed to Diablo, the stallion whickered and tossed his head. With a soft click of his tongue and a soothing touch, Lincoln quieted him. As quickly as the small rebellion was settled, there was still the dread of being discovered skulking among the trees like a voyeur.

But Linsey didn't hear. She didn't see. Satisfied there was no one about, she passed through the door into the light of a house that had been too empty and too dark for too long.

When the house was quiet and only a light in the bedroom that had been Frannie Stuart's still burned, Lincoln steered the stallion toward Belle Reve. After bedding Diablo down for the night, enduring a short command-visit with his father, and refusing the dinner Miss Corey had prepared, he drove to his small pied-à-terre on the outskirts of Belle Terre.

The small city, deeply steeped in old Southern traditions, was the hub of this part of the South Carolina lowcountry. Lincoln's home, situated in a sleepy cul-de-sac on a little-traveled street, was uniquely antebellum, with many of its historic treasures still intact. A single, as the narrow houses with walled and private courtyard gardens were called. In these days when he divided his time between Belle Terre and Belle Reve—with considerably more at the plantation since his father's strokes—the tiny house was all he needed.

An hour later, as he wandered the moonlit courtyard, he realized how much he'd missed the quiet, the solitude. A place that was his alone. Yet the familiar pleasure of it escaped him. His mind was too full, too chaotic. Too filled with memories of Linsey and the boy.

"The boy." Ice clinked against an heirloom crystal glass as he took it from a wrought-iron table. Draining it, he poured another drink from a decanter he'd brought into the garden with him.

"Linsey, the boy, and Brownie." His voice was strained even to himself, and he wondered if one drink had made him drunk. "If it hasn't," he muttered as he lifted the glass before the blaze of an ancient gaslight, "hopefully the next one will."

The boy. The words slashed endlessly through his mind like a broken record he couldn't shut off. *The boy.* It was always that, never more. The child's name was Cade. Yet, for reasons he wouldn't define, Lincoln couldn't bring himself to call Linsey's son by his own name.

Dropping into a chair by the table, he lifted his drink again, watching the play of flames reflected in amber liquid and delicately etched crystal. Fire, the force that changed all their lives. Fire and Oregon. Abruptly Lincoln crashed the glass down with such ferocity it should have shattered, as most of the scotch splashed over the rim.

"Who is he, Linsey? Why is his hair dark when Lucky's was fairer than yours? Who gave him my name?" Drawing a shuddering breath, he whispered, "*Why?* In God's name, why?"

Burying his head in his hands, he didn't speak again. As darkness gathered, beyond the babble of the fountain, the tap of footsteps along the street, and the clink of glass against glass as he poured another drink, the garden was silent.

When he roused, putting away memories he kept locked in the nether regions of his mind, Lincoln didn't know how long he'd sat in the gloom. As he nursed a rare third drink, he didn't care.

Time didn't matter tonight. He was too restless for it to matter. Too confused. Pain lay in his chest like an iron weight. Whatever he did, or didn't do, emotions he didn't understand and didn't know how to deal with tore at him. And with the better part of those three scotches in him— the most he'd had to drink since he and his brothers had given up their carousing, brawling ways—he shouldn't, by damn, be feeling anything.

"Hell," he grumbled, and took another sip, more melted ice than alcohol. "I'm the serious, pragmatic Cade. The logical Cade with all the cool-headed answers. Or so they tell me.

"Yeah," he mocked in harsh sarcasm, "sure I am. Sure I do." Fingers curled into an impotent fist. "So, why not now?"

He was the second of Caesar Augustus Cade's four sons by four wives. The son born of a Scot. Surely she passed along some fine Gaelic practicality in her genes, even if she had died too young to instill it with her teaching. A handsome mouth quirked in a grim smile. "Yep, Gaelic practicality, that's Lincoln Cade."

*Yep.* The boy said that, he remembered.

"The boy." The glass banged down a second time and still survived. Skidding back his chair, Lincoln rose, and from his great height stared down at the perfect haven he'd created. As the Stuart farm had been, this was his place to come when life with a father like Gus became too much. Or when the world weighed too heavily.

"Where do I go now?" he wondered aloud as memories he couldn't exorcise and questions he couldn't answer filled every corner of his heart and mind. When bitterness, black and ugly, joined grief and guilt, how did he deal with them?

"What about the boy?"

His whisper seemed to echo in the small space. Surrounding him, engulfing him in his own voice, asking over and over, *what about the boy?…the boy?*

Laughter from the street broke the illusion. Adult amusement, but in it Lincoln heard the haunting laugh of a child.

But whose child?

Turning to the house, forsaking the garden and his search for peace he knew would elude him for a long time to come, Lincoln knew what he must do. He knew what he would do.

For Lucky, for Linsey, for himself.

For the boy.

# Three

"Look, Mom. Look."

Chuckling, as she made another entry on her growing list of things to do, Linsey wondered what new marvel Cade had discovered. She'd spent the morning taking inventory of needed repairs in the house and barn. Prioritizing each, she balanced their importance against her limited budget while her son resumed an exploration cut short the night before by dinner and bedtime.

Clipping her pen to the small tablet, she smiled again. Recalling that, as he'd drifted off to sleep each of the three nights they'd spent in the old house, Cade had declared the Stuart farm "the bestest place ever," Linsey went to see what new bounty had been added to the exuberant child's list of "bestest" things.

"What is it, Cade?" Blinded by a flood of light, she stepped from the barn. "What have you discovered now?"

Grubby fingers pointed toward the stream. "Company."

Shading her eyes with a hand at her forehead, Linsey

stared at a truck fording the shallow part of the stream as
if it weren't there. Who would come calling so soon? she
wondered. Only the utility companies knew Lucky Stuart's
widow and her son had taken up residence in the old Stuart
farm. Even if the linemen were gossips, it was unlikely
word could spread so fast. She hadn't even stopped in Belle
Terre for groceries.

Cade moved a step toward the house and the truck, eager
for the adventure of meeting someone new. "No, Cade."
Linsey's fingertips settled on his shoulder. "Wait."

"Who is it?" A friendly, fearless child…only her touch
kept him from running to greet the visitor. "Do you
know?"

"No, and I can't think of any reason we might have a
caller so soon," she said. "Unless…" Speculation died on
her lips as she remembered the horse and rider she'd dismissed as a creation of Cade's vivid imagination. As the
truck drew nearer, with a fleeting glimpse and a sense of
the inevitable, she recognized the one man she'd hoped to
avoid.

At least for a little time. Until she had mind, body, and
heart settled and steeped in Lucky's past and in his home.

"Unless what, Mom?" Cade glanced curiously at her.

Linsey had no ready response. But she was saved the
effort as the truck halted before the front steps, its door
swung open, and a tall, dark man emerged. With a sinking
heart, she waited, held motionless by the man, by his magnetism. By memories.

He was tall. Taller than most men, and slender. But when
he reached into the truck for a pair of gloves, the startling
width of his shoulders strained against the seams of his
shirt. His legs were long and provocatively molded by sensible jeans riding low at his waist. Equally sensible low-
heeled boots added an unneeded inch or so to his already
considerable height. His hair, barely visible beneath the
broad brim of his Western hat, was dark and cut short. Yet

it grew in an all-too-familiar defiant swirl over the back of
his neck.

When he turned from the truck, his solemn gaze found
her as he drew on the supple gloves. Refusing to flinch
beneath his wintry stare, even as countless questions raced
through her mind, Linsey realized he was as handsome as
ever. And, a glance at Cade proved, as singularly charis-
matic. As fascinating.

*Don't,* she wanted to cry out. *Don't like him too much.
Don't admire him too much. Don't love him, or he'll break
your young heart, too,* she wanted to warn her son. But
with all that had gone before in her son's young life, she
knew it was too late. It had been too late from the moment
this stalwart, cold-eyed modern-day knight errant emerged
from his gleaming metal steed.

Cade had been taught to love and adore the mystique of
this man all his short life. Now, with his simple act of
walking toward them—gloved, booted, bigger than life
with a tilted Stetson that seemed to touch the sky—Linsey
knew her son would love and adore the flesh-and-blood
Lincoln Cade even more than the image Lucky Stuart had
deliberately created.

"Linsey." Her name spoken in his quiet voice and a
touch at the brim of his hat was Lincoln's only greeting as
he halted before her. Eyes dispassionate and as gray as a
rain-washed sky settled on her face, seeking out every nuance of change. With no altering of his expression, his
study moved on, lingering on hastily banded hair the color
of sunshine, a shirt worn precariously thin, and jeans faded
and more white than blue. Then finally her boots, whose
best days had passed miles before.

His silent perusal complete, his attention flicked down to
Cade. The same dispassion catalogued the sturdy body, the
bright, intelligent face. And hair as dark as Lincoln's own,
grown too long over arching brows. When gray gaze met

gray gaze, one remained steady, unreadable. One stared unabashedly, filled with the first of youthful wonder.

A nod and another touch at the brim of the Stetson accompanied a softly drawled recognition, "Boy."

"Sir." Cade smiled courteously, Linsey's rigorous training not deserting him even in awe.

"Do you know who I am?" Lincoln addressed the spark of recognition in the boy's face. To Linsey, who had never forgotten the cadence of his voice, it held the whet of strain.

"Yes, sir." Cade's head bobbed, confirming Lincoln's speculation as dark hair fell over his eyes. With curled fingers, he brushed it back. "You're Mr. Cade. Once upon a time, when trees burned, you and Lucky jumped out of planes with my mom."

Lincoln visibly relaxed, but didn't turn his attention from the child. "Yes, we did. Once upon a time—a long time."

"I got your name," Cade piped up with a proud lift of his head. "When we lived in Oregon, some of the other kids thought it was funny. But Lucky said two last names is better than one old first name any day of the week."

"*Lucky* said that?" Lincoln was so still, his gaze so intent on the child, even his breathing seemed to cease. His gaze drifted over the dark head, blazoning in his mind the curl a droplet of sweat encouraged at the boy's nape. He considered the tilted chin that would be chiseled, once the gentling softness of youth gave way to maturity. "You call your dad Lucky, do you?"

Throughout the exchange, Linsey had stood like a pillar of stone. Nothing hinted at her tension. Nothing until her half-smothered cry in response to his question.

Lincoln didn't notice, nor did Cade. Both man and boy were locked in a moment in which nothing beyond those steadily held gazes could exist or intrude.

Cade nodded his answer.

"Do you know why, boy?" For reasons he wouldn't try

to explain even to himself, he couldn't call the child by the name he'd been given—his own name. At least not yet.

"Yes, sir." For the first time, a worried expression marred Cade's smooth and even features. Long dark lashes fluttered down to brush his cheeks. In the silence a cricket chirped, and from the depths of the barn a wild cat, likely the descendant of one of Frannie Stuart's pets, growled its displeasure at this disturbance in its domain.

No one paid heed to the complaint. But as if the sound prodded him to answer, Cade drew a long, quiet breath, his frown fading. When the dark cloak of his lashes lifted and he looked at Lincoln, his gaze was calm and sure. In the brave angle of his head a promise of the strong, resolute chin was repeated.

"Yes, sir, I know. But it's a secret. Something Lucky told me. Just me and no one else, man to man."

"Telling would be breaking a promise?" Lincoln suggested, admiration for the boy moving to another level.

"No, sir." The little chin jutted again, but only an increment. "Telling the wrong person at the wrong time would."

Linsey caught back the sound of stifled grief, but Lincoln's focus was riveted on the boy. "Knowing the right person, the right time, and making that decision? That's a big burden for a young boy. Even one as brave as you."

"That's what Lucky said, at first. Then he told me the secret of how I would know."

"This secret, that's part of the promise, too?" Lincoln moved a step closer to the boy, drawn by the unique maturity born of courage. "Lucky taught you that?"

"Yes, sir." Cade's lips began to tremble. Grief crept over his face. "He taught me lots."

Lincoln had struggled to hold himself aloof from this engaging boy who bore his name. Now, seeing stark grief in the trusting eyes, he bent to Cade, the brim of his hat shading them both. "Lucky was a special person. He taught me about courage, too. In fact, he and his mother taught me a lot of things.''

"They did?'' Cade's face brightened. "Lucky taught *you?*''

"Sure.'' Lincoln's hand closed over Cade's shoulder. "What he taught me helped me be as brave as he thought I was. It will be the same for you, too.''

"It will?''

"Just wait, you'll see.'' Lincoln straightened but kept contact with Cade. "Think you could lend me a hand? I brought wood to repair the front steps. I could use your help with it.''

A smile chased grief from Cade's face. "You could?''

"I can manage,'' Lincoln replied. "But an extra pair of hands would be a great help.''

"Lincoln, no.'' Linsey had stood aside, silently watching the first meeting of Lincoln Cade and his namesake. Now she felt compelled to speak out, to buffer the burgeoning camaraderie. "I'm perfectly capable of repairing the step.''

Lincoln didn't turn to Linsey. His grip eased but didn't move from Cade's shoulder. "I know you can, Linsey. But the boy and I are here now.'' A smile flickered over his face as he left the final choice to Cade. "Right, boy?''

Cade's laugh trilled, his grief not forgotten but put aside in a time of healing, youthful glee. "Right, Mr. Cade.''

"Don't, please.'' Linsey moved closer to Lincoln yet dared not touch him. "This isn't a good idea.''

He turned to her then, his gray gaze even colder now than she ever believed it could be. "It's just steps, Linsey. From the look of this place there's plenty more to occupy your time. The boy and I can make quick work of it.'' With a finger he riffled the pages of the tablet she clutched at her breasts. A gesture that could have been intimate, even teasing, but was perfunctory instead. "Then you can get back to your inventory.''

Dismissing her objection, he turned to Cade. "Ready?''

"Yes, sir." The dark head bobbed, the thatch of hair dipped. It was Lincoln who brushed it aside a second before he dropped his own Stetson on the boy's head.

Leaving Linsey with no recourse but to keep silent, the two of them walked away. Lincoln altering his stride to Cade's and Cade's a conscious imitation of Lincoln's. Twice the Stetson toppled. Twice Cade reset it with careful precision.

While a band of fear closed around her heart, Linsey knew Lincoln had done more than soothe Cade's grief, more than bolster a small boy's confidence by enlisting his aid. Whether he knew it or not, whether it was intentional or not, Lincoln Cade had made the first move toward becoming the hero Lucky Stuart had created for Cade. The first move toward making his son irrevocably his own.

"You knew, Linsey," she berated herself bitterly as she watched from the barn door while the tall man from her past and the child of her heart worked together unloading lumber, tools, and even a small garden tractor from the bed of the truck. From the moment she'd promised an ailing, dying Lucky that she would bring her son to the Stuart farm, she knew that one day her path would cross Lincoln's. Just as she'd known that in time the inevitable would happen. "And Lincoln will recognize Cade for who he is."

But first she'd hoped she could... "Could what?" she wondered aloud. "Explain?"

An agitated hand raked through her hair, stripping away the band that held it. Distracted, Linsey let the tie lie unheeded at her feet. For once no impatient hand flung back the cloud of dark gold falling about her shoulders. "How can I explain?" she wondered as she forced herself back to the barn. Surrounded by cool shadows, the inventory forgotten and her mind filled with the vision of the man and boy, she turned away. Moving deeper into muted darkness, she cried softly, "God help me, how?"

* * *

It was Cade's laughter that drew her out of her seclusion and back to the yard. On its heels, barely audible, she heard Lincoln's chuckle. Both ending with the cacophony of a hammer wielded inexpertly. In different circumstances it should have been a pleasant scene. But this was Cade and Lincoln. Because of this day and this meeting, life as Linsey knew it would never be the same. And she was afraid. Very afraid.

Blinking back a rush of tears she dared not let fall, Linsey watched them openly. With the Stetson laid aside, one dark head bent to the other as they conferred, building a bond stronger than any step, leading where no physical structure could go.

Did Lincoln realize? Could he hear what was in Cade's voice? See what was in his eyes and that young, fragile heart?

Did Lincoln care?

"Of course he does." The sound of her own voice startled her. Only then did she realize how long she'd stood idle, her thoughts on the man and the boy and their labor. Lincoln called him "boy," never Cade, but he cared. It was evident in his patience and underlay the impersonal way he spoke. His kindness was innate, unforced. Neither six years, a single, youthful indiscretion at an emotional time, nor the truth would change the man who had been her friend, her family, and, once, her lover.

"Watch, Mom." Cade danced up the steps and down, jumping on each, testing their strength. Once on the ground he ran up again to the porch and launched himself into Lincoln's arms.

Laughing, Lincoln set Cade on his feet. In the sound Linsey heard a sudden restraint. A shiver of caution reminded her Lincoln was ever the pragmatic one, who never rushed into anything. If he felt in his heart it was right, he could walk away from anything, anyone. He had from her. He would from his own son.

"Did you see, Mom? Did you see?"

"I'm sure she saw." Lincoln scooped up the fallen Stetson and pulled it down over Cade's forehead. "Half the county must have heard you. Gus Cade's likely to come bumping down the trail in his wheelchair, yelling that you're scaring his horses out of a year's growth."

Crossing the yard, Linsey saw Cade grow sober. Interpreting a common expression, she knew something Lincoln said sparked his curiosity. The unsuspecting man would be bombarded by the questions of a literal-minded child who took nothing for granted, never assumed. More traits he shared with his father.

"Mr. Gus has horses, but he rides a chair?"

Question number one. Linsey stopped by the porch, crossed her arms and leaned against a support.

Lincoln had moved to inspect the steps, all of which he and Cade had replaced. Sandpaper in hand, he looked up. "What?"

"You said…"

"I know what I said, tiger." Lincoln guessed what had spurred the boy's curiosity. "Actually, the horses pastured at Belle Reve now belong to my brother Jackson. But once Gus kept his own horses and rode them. Then a sickness left his arms and legs too weak to ride or walk. So he uses a wheelchair."

"Where's the trail?"

Lincoln crooked a finger toward the path that wound through scraggly live oaks and palmettos. "Right over there. Lucky and I used it to travel between our houses."

"Between the Stuart farm and Belle Reve," Cade supplied, drawing on the knowledge gleaned during the hours he'd listened to Lucky tell of the countryside, the houses, and his friends. Especially Lincoln. "Lucky never said Mr. Gus rode in a chair."

"He didn't know, Cade," Linsey interjected, her tone as questioning as her son's when her gaze met Lincoln's. "I suppose it happened after Frannie died and we'd settled in Oregon."

Lincoln looked up from sanding the rough edge of a step, his expression unreadable. "Lucky and I had lost touch by then. I knew he and your mom were in Oregon. Or I thought they were. But I didn't know where, exactly."

"You could have looked, couldn't you?" Cade picked up the block of wood Lincoln had covered in sandpaper for him and scrubbed at an imaginary rough spot.

With the boy and the steps between them, Linsey waited for his answer. "Yes." His expression was brooding, but Cade couldn't see. "I could have looked, but I didn't think he wanted me to."

"I guess not," the boy agreed. "He didn't want anybody to know he was sick, too."

"Lucky was sick?" Catching the busy hand, stopping it, Lincoln waited until Cade looked up at him. "For very long?"

Cade started his habitual nod, caught himself and the Stetson perched precariously over his forehead, then chose words instead. "A long, long, *long* time."

"The letter said he fell." Lincoln directed the oblique question toward Linsey.

Searching for the simplest way to describe a horrible and inexorably debilitating disease, she hesitated long enough that Cade answered in her stead.

"Being sick's what made him fall. His arms and legs didn't work too good no more, just like Mr. Gus."

Cade picked up the sander, scrubbing too diligently over a step that was already smooth. Linsey stretched an arm across the staircase, and with her fingertips stroked the swirling hair on the back of his neck. A tender gesture that spoke more than words.

"How long is a long, long, long time, Linsey?" If Lincoln's expression had been grim before, with this discovery his look took it ten times farther.

With her arms drawn tightly against her again, Linsey stifled a painful memory. "Two years for the worst of it. Longer for the less insidious progression. Before you ask why you weren't told, remember how Lucky was. You were so strong, and he wanted to be like you, but he couldn't. So he made up for what he lacked with pure courage. He didn't want your help, Lincoln. Nor mine, until he had no choice. Even then, there were days..."

When she paused to gather her control, with new knowledge Lincoln saw beyond the surface fatigue of months to the deep, soul-searing weariness of years. Yet she could laugh and dance with her son on a ramshackle porch at sunset in a strange land.

With a toss of her head, Linsey gathered in her emotions, a gesture that sent her hair flying. As the morning sun struck a rainbow of shades of gold within its depths, Lincoln was reminded of a lioness. A proud lioness who fought for her mate and her cub.

An ache settled deep in his chest as he wondered if once she would have fought as courageously for him.

"There were days," she began again, tentatively, unaware of the subtle shift in his regard. "Days when he was stronger, when he lived on determination alone, accomplishing amazing feats." Throughout the revelation, Linsey's stare was vague, unfocused. Now her head lifted, her gaze narrowed sharply on Lincoln. "If you remember any one thing about Lucky, remember his courage, and that he died as bravely as he lived."

Lincoln found the blunt answer unsettling, too brief. He had a hundred questions, a thousand. But none for the boy's ears. "All right." Meaningless words. Nothing was all right. Nothing about this was clear. Nothing was resolved.

Casting a look at Linsey that promised there would be more, Lincoln turned to Cade. "Looks to me like you've finished that step. In fact, they all look good. Smooth and sturdy. No one's going to fall through them or catch a splinter. Now we need to do something about the yard. What do you think?''

Cade squinted up at him, one sawdust-covered hand flattened over the crown of the hat. "We could mow it down."

"Mow it down, huh?" Lincoln studied the yard as if considering the suggestion. "You mean with the tractor."

"Yep."

Lincoln almost smiled then, remembering the conversation between mother and son the night before. "Looks like a pretty big job. Think you could ride shotgun? A man never knows when he might need some help."

"Could I?" Gray eyes that had grown brighter, gleamed like new silver. "Like on a stagecoach?"

"Will you promise to be very still and hold on?" Lincoln watched the little head bob. The hat toppled, and he scooped it from the ground. "Okay, partner. Now, if your mom will lend us a couple of sheets of paper from her tablet, I'll fix your hat so it will stay on. Then we'll get on with our work and she can see about her own chores. Deal?"

"Deal," Cade said, and watched wide-eyed as Lincoln folded and refolded the papers Linsey supplied, tucked them inside the band of his hat, then set it firmly on Cade's head.

"There." With an expert touch he adjusted the hat at just the right angle. "How's that?"

"My hat?" Cade whispered in wonder. "Is it really mine?"

"Sure. You don't think I'm tricking you, do you?" With a hand curled around the boy's neck, Lincoln led him to his mother. "Say goodbye and tell your mom not to worry, for we're going to cut the trail as well and it will take some time. While we're at the far end, we might as well stop over at Belle Reve. Maybe look at some horses, have some lunch. Would you like that?"

"Horses! Can I, Mom?" Cade practically danced in excitement. The hat didn't budge. "Please, can I?"

Cade asked. Lincoln hadn't. Linsey knew that if she was adamant, her refusal would be respected...and Cade would be heartbroken. "Okay, okay. But before you go, Cade should run inside and wash his hands."

"His hands are fine, Linsey. If he washes them, they'll just get dirty again. We do have water and soap at Belle Reve."

"I want him to wash up now, Lincoln." She'd kept virtually silent and had held her temper all day. Now her voice was harsh, her challenging stare unwavering.

"Do as your mother says, champ." Lincoln didn't look away from Linsey as they faced each other like prizefighters. "Make it quick—we've a lot of grass to cut."

With an exuberant cry and a hug for his mother, Cade rushed up the stairs and over the porch. The door banged shut before Linsey spoke. "What do you think you're doing, Lincoln Cade? Waltzing in here like you own the place. Enticing Cade with horses. Courting him like—"

"Like a friend who promised his father he would take care of you? Which, in my estimation, means the boy, as well." Cade moved closer, watching the kaleidoscopic shades of gold shimmering in her hair, filling his lungs with the fragrance of Frannie Stuart's wild rose concoction. The scent that still lingered in the house. Linsey's life paralleled Frannie's, and she was as strong. Wild roses seemed right for her.

"I won't hurt him, Linsey," he said in a voice barely above a whisper. "Whatever happens here, I won't hurt him."

"Whatever happens?" He was so close, if she caught a deep breath the tips of her breasts would touch his chest. If he leaned down only a little, she could run her fingers through the wealth of his hair and perhaps draw his lips down to hers.

But she didn't catch a long breath, and his rigid posture didn't bend. Her fingers were curled in tight fists by her side. Instead of softening in a kiss, her lips were clenched. Lincoln might be a friend, he might be her benevolent enemy. In either case, she must hold herself aloof, turning blind eyes to the mystique that had already enchanted her son.

"Why are you really here? What do you want, Lincoln?"

His gaze was as silver as Cade's, and it was riveted on her. "I don't know, Linsey. But I'll be back tomorrow and the next day and the next. And every other day, until I do."

"No."

"Yes." His gloved fingers circled the wrist of the hand she'd raised, not to strike him, but to ward him off. Linsey didn't struggle, nor did he relent. "I love this place, it was more home to me than Belle Reve. Lucky was like a brother, and Frannie was the mother I never had. For them, for the boy, I'm going to put it back in shape. Make it a home he can be proud of."

"Your practice…"

Keeping hold of her wrist, his fingertips measuring her racing pulse, he quirked his lips in a caricature of a smile. "That won't work, sugar. My partner's been trying to persuade me to take time off for months. Now I have. I'll be here every day, all day, for as long as it takes. Just like I said."

"I don't need you," Linsey cried in desperation, not really sure what frightened her most about Lincoln's plan. "What's needed here, I can do."

"Can you?" Releasing her, Lincoln stepped back, his look harsh as it traveled the same path with the same thoroughness as it had when he first arrived. A look that tarried long on her lips and the straining of her breasts against a shirt worn as thin as gauze. "With what? You're broke, Linsey. Every sign is there."

"So what if I am? Until I find work, what I can't afford we'll do without. I will not take your charity, Lincoln Cade."

"It won't be charity."

"What name would you give it?" she flung at him.

"Call it my gift to Lucky for—" Lincoln faltered.

"For what?" Linsey taunted. "What should I call it?"

"Try my thanks to the Stuarts for my life."

The door banged, breaking the tension but not ending it. "I'm ready," Cade called out. "I washed my face, too, Mom."

Linsey turned toward Cade. "That's good, tiger."

It was Lincoln who ended the standoff by moving to the steps and catching Cade in the midst of another flying leap. Without an added word, he offered the boy's cheek for his mother's kiss, and as quickly as that, Linsey had a day alone.

As she watched their retreat, Cade's arms locked firmly around Lincoln's neck, she knew it would be a day of worry.

# Four

Cade's giggle drew Linsey to the kitchen window. A familiar sound since Lincoln had walked into his life weeks before.

Smiling in spite of nagging worries, she stood on tiptoe, leaning over the sink to get a better view beyond the sparkling window. For her effort, she was bemused as always by the powerful presence of the quintessential male. But not just any man or just one. Though she was reminded constantly that Lincoln's unfailing presence was disturbing enough, life on the Stuart farm was not meant to be even that simple.

Instead, the power was fourfold and daunting, for her backyard was filled with Cades—with Lincoln and his brothers. Men who had been only familiar names in the years she and Lucky and Lincoln had been close. Now all four Cades were here, as they had been for days, each filling his own space with his own particular charisma. Each contributing some area of skill and expertise.

Adams, the oldest of the four, in response to Lincoln's call for help, had drawn his crews from an antebellum town house he was restoring on the outskirts of Belle Terre. Under his direction a number of skilled artisans—carpenters, plumbers, electricians, and painters—had made quick work of what they did best. Restoring yet another pair of historic derelicts fallen victim to time and circumstance.

Of the house and barn, the house had been the first order of business. Anything broken, loose, rotted or just plain cranky had been repaired, replaced or soothed. The ancient exterior gleamed with a fresh layer of paint and the tin roof with its first. Stylish, historically correct shutters replaced the sagging boards that had served originally. Cobblestone walks and borders, and fences to keep deer from flower and vegetable gardens had been resurrected.

But it was the interior that astonished Linsey. With a small knowledge of furnishings gleaned from her travels in her lonely, footloose days, she had recognized that there had been good pieces left to time and chance in the old house. Abandoned yet protected, she believed strongly, by its proximity to Belle Reve and by fear of the wrath of the Cades. All of whom seemed to revere the farm for the woman who had lived there.

Once Frannie Stuart's unsuspected treasures were refurbished by Adams's skilled crews, she realized they were more than a reflection of Frannie's taste, more than merely valuable. Many were antiques of the first quality. A part of Lucky's heritage. His legacy to the child he'd loved and made his own.

Inspired by the discovery of marvelous family treasures, the artisans' work had become equally more meticulous. As a fitting backdrop for this bounty, fresh coats of paint had been applied to every wall, countertops were replaced, and floors repaired and refurbished with such speed, it made her breathless remembering. There was more to do.

But, wisely, Adams had suggested Linsey should make the more personal choices, then had left them to her.

Jackson, the fiery one, third in birth order and noted horse breeder, had seen to the land. Drafting Lincoln, along with his own people, he worked with fences enclosing more than a hundred acres of pasture and timber. Though appreciative, Linsey wondered what use she would make of those acres. Jackson offered the solution. By mutual agreement she would have an unexpected source of income from fees he would pay for grazing rights.

Jefferson, the youngest, whose quiet ways and gentle smile had set her more at ease than any of the Cades, had taken an old orchard and the landscaping as his project. Peach, apple, and pear trees were pruned. Pecan trees were squirrelproofed. A small vineyard became less like a jungle. Jefferson had even offered suggestions and help for plants for the house and gardens.

Miss Corey had been an absentee contributor to the cause. The housekeeper of Belle Reve, a woman Linsey knew only by reputation, dispatched her kitchen staff regularly with three hot meals each day. Morning, noon, and evening in a splendid, rainless period, Miss Corey's fare was served on tables made of boards and sawhorses set beneath centuries-old live oak.

Cade had been beside himself with the excitement of the ongoing picnic. After the seclusion of Lucky's illness, then the loneliness of their travel following his death, the little boy reveled in the companionship. Blossoming, as any outgoing five-year-old would, beneath the shower of attention.

In the weeks the collective effort required, Lincoln worked harder than anyone, but kept a watchful distance. Only a few days into the concerted project, Linsey realized that if Jackson hadn't commandeered his brother to help in the far regions of Stuart land, Lincoln would have volunteered.

''Or found another chore equally as separate,'' she spoke

softly, her words echoing in the unnatural silence of the house.

At first she'd been grateful. But just as quickly she'd discovered that no matter how distant or unintrusive he tried to be, she was unceasingly aware of him. Just knowing Lincoln was near left her speechless and tense.

Because of churning emotions, though she managed to be pleasant and appreciative, Linsey could never relax enough to become a part of the congenial interaction of the bothers and the crews. With so much happening, and so much accomplished, she knew she should be accustomed to the bedlam of the blistering pace, and certainly the teasing. Especially now that Adams's and Jackson's crews had returned to Belle Terre and only the Cades themselves remained.

Yet after weeks of clamoring activity and having witnessed much of the constant, good-natured jousting between the brothers, she still could neither trust Lincoln's reasons for this generosity nor participate in the camaraderie.

Linsey admitted the fault lay in her. She'd never had anything remotely resembling a family. At least not before the years she had been smoke-jumping partners with Lucky and Lincoln.

"They were my family." Startled by the wistful tone, she rebuffed the memory, determined she wouldn't go there. She wouldn't dwell on what might have been. Her concerns were here and now. Cade first. Then Lincoln.

Cade giggled again. Linsey's focus returned to the pandemonium in the yard and by the barn. She watched Jackson scoop the boy up by the waistband of his jeans, then pause in midstride to rescue an oversize boot that tumbled from one small foot. Lincoln's boots, confiscated by Cade when his hero returned from the field and exchanged them for footwear better suited for clambering over the tin roof of the barn.

Boot tucked under one arm, Cade dangling from the other, Jackson jogged to the barn, where he passed his wriggling burden into Adams's care. The eldest of the Cades and her son disappeared into the hayloft, and Linsey turned away from the window.

Taking up a forgotten cup of tea, her fingers absently caressing the delicate china, she stared into the cooling liquid. Cade loved Jackson for his flamboyance, Jefferson for his boy-like quality, and Adams for his patient willingness to answer endless questions. But it was to Lincoln he turned. Lincoln he mimicked. Lincoln he worshiped and loved. Lincoln to whom he belonged.

Yet Lincoln said nothing.

But he knew. Each of them knew. It was there in their eyes when they looked at Cade. But no one spoke of it, and no one questioned as they waited. As Linsey waited...for Lincoln.

"Linsey."

With a start, she turned, losing her grasp on the cup that shattered at her feet. "Oh, no." She went to her knees, gathering the jagged shards with shaking hands. "Oh, no," she cried again. "It was so beautiful."

Lincoln's fingers closed over hers, taking the remnants of china from her. "It's just a cup."

She shook her head, hardly aware that Lincoln's hands were empty and had closed again over hers. "You don't understand." She lifted eyes bright with tears to his. "It was *hers,* Lucky's mother's. An heirloom of the Stuart family."

"But still just a cup." He drew her to her feet and would have reached for his handkerchief, but her tears had vanished. This was the Linsey he knew. Tenderhearted to a fault, too tough for copious tears. "Frannie's gone, Linsey. The cup is yours."

She only shook her head as he led her to a chair by the

table. "Wait here." There was a peculiar hoarseness in his voice. "I'll get a cloth and something for the cut."

Linsey watched him go. A broad-shouldered, virile man who moved with the surety of one familiar with the house. Of course he was. Linsey wondered what it would have been like to be a part of his life as Lucky and Frannie Stuart had been; her heart ached with loss of the man that boy had become.

A boy like Cade.

Biting her lips to keep them from trembling, she looked away from the hall that was empty now. Bowing her head, letting her gaze fall on twined hands, she realized she was bleeding more than she thought from the cut she'd hardly noticed. That would explain the look on Lincoln's face, the sound of his voice—concern, not caring.

Mutely Linsey sat listening to laughter filtering in from the yard, Cade's giggle resounding like a bell among the deep tones of the men. Her son was happy here. Happier than he'd ever been. But would it last? Could it, when she admitted to Lincoln what she must? When he hated her for what she'd done.

Raising her uninjured hand, Linsey shielded her eyes, wishing she could shield Cade as easily. With thumb and forefinger she massaged the muscles at her temples, drawn taut and tender from constant and escalating tension.

The scent of fresh air, cedar, and soap surrounded her as Lincoln knelt before her, a basin of water, a cloth, and a tube of salve in his hands. Setting them aside, he drew her hand from her face. "Are you all right?" A small smile touched his lips. "You haven't grown squeamish at the sight of your own blood, have you?"

"No," she began, and discovered her voice shook as he exchanged one hand for another, cradling her wounded palm in his. She tried again more forcefully. "Of course not."

"Then what…?" He let the question drift away, leaving her to fill in the explanation.

Linsey kept her gaze from his as she stared at their joined hands. Lincoln's were large and strong and tanned. Hardened by the demands of his veterinary practice and his labors at Belle Reve, yet so gentle. Hers were much smaller. One might think delicate, were they not reddened and raw from cleansers and scrubbing. Not a pretty sight, with broken and unkempt nails. Yet Lincoln didn't seem to notice or care.

"Linsey?" he prompted when she didn't answer. "You're not still worried about the cup, are you?"

"I shouldn't have been so careless." Grateful for any opening, she continued, "Someone took wonderful care with the china in the past. In less than a month I wreak havoc."

"I doubt *havoc* is the word." As he spoke he opened her fingers, exposing the slice that crossed her palm. With a cloth and warm, soapy water, he cleansed the cut, applied the salve she'd bought only a few days before, then circled her hand with gauze he taped in place. "There, that should suffice."

Linsey waited for Lincoln to release her and move away. When he continued to kneel at her feet, keeping her hand in his, she lifted her head and found him studying her through a veil of lashes. Their gazes collided, yet neither spoke. The gray of his eyes was rimmed with black, then splashed with bits of silver. She was struck again by how beautiful they were. How enigmatic, betraying nothing of what he felt or thought.

Even in dread of that inevitable moment when he would speak the truth, she felt the power of his magnetism, the subtle sensuality that was so much an inherent part of him he was hardly aware of it. Lincoln had been her friend, her champion, her first lover. Soon the memories of what they'd shared would be tarnished. Whatever he'd felt for her that single day in the midst of raging wildfire would be lost in anger and enmity.

Yet, waiting beneath his solemn gaze, she felt the first flush of feverish need as familiar and wanton as in that never-forgotten perilous time. Need as unthinking, as reckless, drawing her gaze to his lips. Waking memories of kisses that beguiled, caresses that seduced in tender torment.

Need that could only lead to heartbreak again.

Cold fear gripped her. Lincoln hadn't wanted her before. He'd walked away as if making love with her was no more than aberrant, meaningless lust born of a desperate moment. Yet he could still make her want him with an impersonal touch. In that lay destruction, for herself. Perhaps for Cade.

She mustn't fall under Lincoln's spell again. Catching an uneven breath, seeking strength that had meant her survival before, Linsey vowed she wouldn't.

Taking her hand from his, refusing to care that his fingertips brushed her thigh, she muttered, "I could have managed, but thanks."

"Yes." Lincoln withdrew abruptly and stood looking down at her. "You can manage, can't you?" Something she couldn't fathom, perhaps anger, perhaps melancholy, flashed in his eyes, then vanished as quickly. "You always have."

Her chin tilted with the spirit that had meant her survival too many times in her life. "I try, Lincoln."

She thought he would speak. Instead, his face without expression, he turned and walked to the door. Pausing there, his back to her, he seemed reluctant to go. As if there was more he would say. But again he said nothing as he opened the door and stepped through it to the porch.

Sounds of laughter that had seeped past walls and windows rushed in, teasing, enticing, making a mockery of the solitude she'd chosen as her armor. She dared not let what she felt for Lincoln's brothers go beyond neighborly gratitude. She dared not like them or need their approval. But like Lincoln, neither Adams nor Jackson nor Jefferson took an unspoken no for an answer. Like Lincoln, each in his own way was irresistible.

"My brothers are waiting," Lincoln said from the door. "Their work here is finished. They'd like to say goodbye."

Linsey looked away, her gaze falling on her hands clasped in her lap. "How long?"

"Before you have to brave the departing lions?"

Linsey knew the teasing remark was made in an effort to lessen her obvious disquiet. But so long as there was this impasse between them, nothing could give her ease.

"They won't bite, you know," he said, before she could think of a response. "They don't want polite, undying gratitude. They came to help because you're Lucky's wife. They stayed because they like you. And because of the boy."

*The boy.* Linsey searched her memory, seeking a time he'd called Cade by name. Perhaps he had, but only rarely, and the effort to remember made her head hurt and her throat and her heart. The cut across her palm had begun to throb as well. She wanted to have done with this day. With the Cades and their kindnesses. Kindnesses she must repay, in time, with the revelation of deception.

Dear God, she must have done with that, too. Ending this game of cat and mouse. She would, she must. But first, today. The last day the Cades would fill her yard and her son's heart with laughter. "When will they be leaving?"

"Soon."

Linsey rose from her seat to face him. "I don't want to say goodbye looking like this." An unsteady hand brushed at bloodstains she'd just discovered. "I'll freshen up and change, then be right out."

"I'll wait." Lincoln stepped back through the door, filling the room more with his presence than with his size.

"Don't." The denial burst from her. Though he wasn't

close and there was nothing threatening in his demeanor, Linsey backed away, her bandaged hand a white slash across the darkness of her shirt as she clutched it to her breasts. "There's no need."

"I said I would wait, Linsey. And I will." He moved farther into the room, closing the door behind him. Drawing out a chair by the table where she'd been sitting, he waited by it. A gentleman never sat while a lady stood.

"Lincoln…" she began, then broke off, realizing she had no reasonable argument. When he cast a questioning look at her, she frowned and muttered, "I'll change."

When she was gone, closing the bedroom door emphatically behind her, Lincoln still stood. He didn't move until he recognized the faint hiss of the shower. Rather than sit, he strolled down the hall, stopping at the door of the bedroom that once was Lucky's and belonged now to Cade.

*Cade.* Lincoln couldn't think of him as boy or tiger or champ or anything so casual as he went uninvited into the small room filled with boyish treasures. Beyond fresh paint on the walls and new, colorful linens on the narrow bed, little was changed. Lucky's baseball trophies had been polished and still lined the shelves. With those of his own still among them. Cade was young yet for baseball, but soon.

Lincoln's photograph with a young Diablo had been moved to the bedside table—the place of honor. In honor of himself or the horse? he wondered. Then he laughed at the arrogance when he remembered Cade's fascination with horses.

Tucked beside the yellowing photograph was a smaller framed snapshot of Cade and Lucky. Taking it from its place, Lincoln was careful not to disturb a bird's nest, a tangle of string, and a feather the boy was convinced belonged to an eagle. In the photo Cade stood by Lucky's chair, his face filled with pride for the minnow-size fish that dangled at the end of a cane pole. A lush, green riverbank was barely visible in the background.

For a long while Lincoln studied the dark-haired, gray-eyed child with the infectious gap-toothed grin. A boy too tall for tattered jeans that left his ankles exposed, and a T-shirt that barely skimmed his waist. Intelligence brimmed in those bright eyes, and Lincoln knew a dozen questions could rattle from his lips on any given subject in a matter of minutes.

"Why do horses have manes?" "What does a turtle see in his shell?" Lincoln recalled recent gems. "How high is it to the top of the sky." "Will the eagle fall if he loses too many feathers?"

"How did you answer the impossible questions, Lucky?" he asked the image of the man who had been his friend for most of his life. A man he hardly recognized. The Lucky Stuart he remembered was never so tall as he, but broader, sturdier, with supple muscles. The Lucky pictured in blurred, grainy color was thin, nearly emaciated, and pale. His blond hair was streaked with lighter strands of white. And what was once a thick, unruly mop had thinned and lay plastered against his skull.

At a glance his grin for the camera was cheerful. But for one who had known him so well, it was strained, forced. As if the muscles of his face hadn't the strength to lift the sagging, yellow-tinged flesh into a true smile.

"What happened?" Lincoln wondered aloud. "And what in the name of all that's holy was a man in this condition doing on a slope threatening to slide?"

"He was saving two children."

Linsey stood in the doorway. Though the bandage was still dry, her hair was damp and curling around her shoulders. The scent of soap and shampoo blended with the haunting fragrance of Frannie Stuart's wild roses. Lincoln realized again how much the scent became her. How right it was that she should be here, no matter what trouble might smolder between them.

"How did you know there was a slide warning?" Linsey

asked. Crossing to stand beside him, she showed no surprise at finding him in Cade's room.

"Jackson told me."

With a half smile Linsey finished, "And Cade told him."

Lincoln didn't bother to verify the source of the story. There was no need. "How does the threat of a slide figure into the accident? I was led to believe Lucky died as the result of injuries sustained in a fall. I assumed in the line of his duties with the park service."

"There was a slide warning issued for hillsides and mountains near our cabin. Not uncommon for the area after protracted rains cut thousands of sloughs in the unstable terrain. With the warning and some common sense, at this location no one would have been in any danger. But, like any slide, even the small ones, it could have been lethal for anyone who triggered it or was in its path," Linsey explained.

She spoke knowledgeably about the subject. Lincoln wasn't surprised, for he knew from reports resulting from his search for her that she'd spent time as a ranger with the National Park Service. There was more he wanted to know and understand, but he didn't interrupt or question. This was the most she'd said on any subject voluntarily—the first time she'd spoken without guardedly choosing her words. Hopefully, it meant the walls she'd erected had begun to crumble.

She could be a spirited woman and a frightened kitten all in one. It was the woman and the fighter he wanted when he brought the plan he'd set into motion to fruition.

Linsey felt the solemn weight of his gray gaze moving over her, then biding on her lips. Lincoln still had the power to disturb her, excite her. In the past he hadn't understood his charm or his magnetism...now he knew it too well. She found it an effort not to stumble over her words as she continued Lucky's story.

"Two children from the neighborhood played hooky

from school. They were hiding from their parents when
they strayed too close to the danger zone. I'd been called
back to the park, but Lucky was observing the area with
binoculars. He saw them.''

"He was like this." A dark finger touched the withered
legs in the photograph. "And he went for them instead of
calling for help?''

"He called," Linsey explained, her voice roughened by
grief. "But he felt there was no time to spare." Her composure slipped, only for a moment. "Lucky wanted to go.''

His gaze returning to the photograph, Lincoln waited.

"He crawled, Lincoln. No one understood how he made
it. But he did and even managed to coax them to climb to
higher, stable ground. The little one needed more help than
he had energy to give. Somehow he found the last reserves
to do what he had to. They were safe when his strength
failed.''

"He fell then?" As he read the answer on her face, Lincoln saw that she had grown pale with telling the tragedy.
He had only a few more questions, then this could all be
put behind them. Lucky wouldn't be forgotten, but Linsey,
Cade, and he would go on with their lives.

"He wasn't part of the park service anymore. My guess
is he hadn't been for some time." Lincoln looked at the
photograph, a gaunt travesty of the Lucky he remembered.
"He was too sick.''

"With MS, primary progressive multiple sclerosis. It's
estimated that only 15 percent of those who suffer from the
disease have this vicious, fast-moving form." Linsey let the
awful truth hang between them like the dying knell of a
bell. Then, quietly, she continued, "Lucky was one of
them.''

"How long, Linsey?''

"How long did he suffer its effects? Six years. In a
milder, unrecognized form, probably longer.''

Lincoln recalled a day in an Oregon hospital. Lucky

seemed too quiet, as if he was disturbed by more than the
burns that were an occupational hazard for smoke jumpers.
Later Lincoln attributed it to life-changing decisions his
friend had made. Decisions that changed all their lives.
''That means…''

''That Lucky found out while he was in the hospital following the Oregon fire that his fatigue was more than the
effect of grieving over his mother's death,'' Linsey finished
for him. With probing fingers, she absently massaged the
soreness left at her temple by tension and clenched teeth.

''It was that simple?''

Linsey's lips tilted in a parody of a smile. The soft glare
from the window reflected on the green in her eyes, and
the hint of blue seemed to fade for a moment. ''Nothing's
ever that simple with MS. Later there were tests, an MRI,
lumbar punctures, and anything else the doctors could
dream up.''

Lincoln watched the play of changing light over her face.
A face that had grown so pale the brilliance of her eyes
was mesmerizing. Were they green? Blue? How many
times had he wondered what her mood would be, and the
color it would turn that beautiful gaze? How many times
had Lucky teased her, calling her eyes the barometer of her
temperament?

*Lucky.*

The room seemed too small, too crowded with memories
and pain. The low rumble of his brothers' conversation
grew more distinct as they finished the last of their chores
and gathered at the porch steps, waiting for Linsey.

Returning the frame to its place of honor, he took Linsey's arm. ''My brothers still wait. Shall we join them?''

The cotton sundress she'd chosen swirled like silk
around her knees as she turned to walk with him. His fingers were firm and warm against the soft skin of her inner
arm, guiding her. In the narrow hallway, Lincoln drew her
close, his knuckles inadvertently brushing the swell of the

side of her breast. A touch waking desire that slumbered forever within her. Kindling needs lying in wait barely beneath the surface.

Linsey's head was spinning, her heart racing. She wanted to pull away and dismiss all he'd done for her as neighborly kindness given in honor of friendship. She wanted to forget his gentleness as he bandaged her hand. The gallant concern, the look that almost made her believe he cared.

She wanted to lie to herself and, with the lie, make it true that she didn't still love him and that with a touch he couldn't make her want him. That, like a fool, she wouldn't still want him when there might be loathing in his eyes.

She wanted desperately to believe each and all of these. She couldn't. For days, even as she'd avoided him as exactingly as he had her, she'd felt as if they were hurtling down some unmarked path. Something in the way Lincoln looked at her and touched her warned that after this day nothing would be the same.

"Linsey."

The slight pressure of his fingers gliding down her arm drew her to a halt. His family waited beyond the door, and she tried not to let her dread show in the gaze she lifted to his. Incredibly he smiled down at her and, with a callused finger, traced the line of her throat, tilting her face another degree. Bending to her, he brushed her lips with his. Once, twice, in a whisper of a kiss. For all its gentleness, a kiss that branded her, promising more.

She was still staring at him, confusion buffeting her like a hurricane, when he folded her trembling fingers in the crook of his arm.

"They're Cades, mortal men, and no threat to you. Neither of them would hurt you or presume to judge you, Linsey." Lincoln's lips curled in a small smile.

"Nor will I, my love." He offered the assurance quietly as, in an uncomprehending instant, he swept her through the door, to the porch, to face his family.

# Five

A smattering of applause drifted across the clearing when Linsey stepped onto the porch with Lincoln. Startled, her hand gripping his arm, her eyes downcast, she stopped short. For what could only have been a little time but spun into forever, she hesitated, gathering her courage.

Lincoln stood patiently, offering strength and support in the power of his touch. When the applause faded, drawing a quivering breath, she lifted her gaze to those assembled in the yard. Amid the order and renewal gradually evolved out of chaos and disrepair, she discovered the last gathering, and the last meal for the Cades on Stuart land, had become a celebration. One with the style and thoughtfulness she'd come to expect from this extraordinary family.

One by one she looked at them. At men who had been kinder than she thought possible, for reasons she didn't understand. Each had found the time to wash away the evidence of this day's labor. Crisp, pressed shirts were tucked into fresh jeans. Boots had been wiped clean, if not polished. And hats held in hands were newly brushed and shaped.

It was only after seeing his brothers and the care and pride they'd taken in this moment that Linsey realized Lincoln had done the same. When he'd come to her in the house, she'd looked at him, yet in her state of mind and with the added distress of the shattered cup and the cut, she hadn't truly seen him.

She'd been aware of him. Perhaps too aware of the mingled, masculine scents to see that his hair was darkened and damp. Or that his shirt and jeans and boots were immaculate without a speck of sawdust, paint, or other evidence of any of a number of duties he'd likely undertaken in the course of the day. Nor had she realized until this instant that while his gloves were tucked in his belt, his second-best hat—worn now that Cade had his best—was nowhere insight.

The Cades had labored weeks for Lucky's widow. Today the care, the decorum, the welcome, was for her. For Linsey. As if in this they were showing her that she mattered.

"Thank you," she said to Lincoln, knowing it was enough for him. It would be enough for all the Cades, she was certain, even as she spoke to each in turn.

"Adams."

Lean and sun darkened, with silver beginning to dust his dark-brown hair, the first of Gus Cade's sons stood in the pooling shade of an oak. A stunning woman—with pale-brown hair and a lovely smile the dusky shelter of sprawling, moss-covered tree limbs couldn't dim—stood at his side. From one brief meeting Linsey remembered this was Eden, Adams's wife. From his sporadic conversations in his attempts to put her at ease while he worked with his crews on the interior of the farmhouse, Linsey knew this lovely lady was the first and only female to beguile and captivate one of the courtly, elusive Cades.

"This house represents all I've never had—a family,

roots, a history. Thank you for bringing it alive, for making it the home it should be," she said to Adams. "A home for Cade and for me. I hope one day you don't regret what you've done for us."

"The little I've done has been my pleasure, Linsey. I won't regret it." A gallant half bow accompanied Adams's acknowledgment of her gratitude. As he straightened, a fleeting glance meeting Eden's made it exquisitely apparent even to a relative stranger that Adams was truly captivated.

Linsey remembered a time she thought Lincoln might look at her as his brother looked at Eden. A look that reminded her of what she would never have. For only a fool could doubt that while Adams honored and respected all women, it was Eden he found utterly bewitching. Eden with whom he was shamelessly in love. Eden who made his life complete.

Adams Cade was content as few were. The contentment his manner warned he knew was lacking in Linsey Stuart. The peace she knew he would wish for the woman he thought her.

In his arms was proof, beautiful and bittersweet, of love shared, even returned tenfold. A baby girl, a striking replica of her father, tugged at his hair and explored an ear, then leaned to trail kisses across a face so much like her own.

Noelle, the miracle child. The baby modern science predicted could never be. Evidence, as with Cade, of the powerful virility and dominant genes of the Cades.

Beyond the miracle of her birth, this beautiful little girl was witness of the power of love. Yes, Linsey thought as Noelle turned to chatter at the world with her father's smile, this child was about love.

Because it hurt to see what she'd lost, Linsey turned away, but not before she whispered without thinking, "But how could I lose what was never mine?"

Lincoln leaned near. His lips brushed her hair. "Something wrong, love?"

Linsey was too distraught to hear. Understanding only that he'd spoken, she shook her head, leaving it to him to interpret the gesture as her answer. Or that she had no answer.

A pace or two away from Adams and his family, Jackson lounged in the sun, its rays turning his close-cut auburn hair to flame. In his tales to Cade, Lucky had described the third brother perfectly as the hotheaded soft touch. Quick to anger, quicker to laugh, to tease, to love. A man whose brute strength cloaked an amazing cognition and the tenderest of hearts.

Linsey had discovered the truth of that heart from afar time and again with Cade. She saw it now in the softening of his expression. Even while his brilliant blue-green gaze filled with mischief as it raked over her, then Lincoln, and back again to her. A wink acknowledged her thanks, as a quirk curled his lips into a knowing grin.

Certain Jackson had seen through the charade she played, that in this moment he'd read what was in her mind and heart, Linsey felt the beginning of a flush stain her throat.

"Jackson." In her hurry to deflect his notice from the tension she felt, she rushed into an enumeration of all he'd done. "I can't thank you enough for restoring the pastures and fences, and the barn, and…" She lost her train of thought, then resolutely gathered her wits. "Especially for making the Stuart farm truly a farm again, as it should be."

"Well, love, after that pretty speech, I'd like to take credit for every improvement of the pastures, every new and repaired fence." Jackson's impudent grin, still no more than a tilt of one corner of his mouth and a crinkle of his eyes, abandoned Linsey to taunt Lincoln. "But I'd be a liar. Lincoln worked harder than anyone and did more than his share. If I didn't know what a good, upstanding fellow he is, I would say he worked as if the hounds of hell were gnawing on him.

"I could say you don't owe me anything for being a

good neighbor, Linsey. Especially since I stand to gain more from your pastures than you. But considering Lincoln's bad mood, and that I had to put up with him during this undertaking, I'll just say, you're quite welcome. Not for the pastures or the work, but for taking him off your hands, at least for a while.''

Ignoring Lincoln's gruff groan of denial, his little speech done, Jackson let that same perceptive study move over them again. Determined the lazy scrutiny and sly banter wouldn't unnerve her, with the poise she could manage, Linsey shifted her attention to Jefferson.

The youngest Cade stood apart from his brothers. He was leaner than Jackson or Adams, but not so tall as Lincoln. His hair was neither close-cropped, nor so neatly groomed as his brothers'. Instead, it was thicker and longer and banded at his nape by a circle of turquoise. Varying shades of blond gleamed in contrast to the darker hues of Jackson's and Adams's and Lincoln's.

Jefferson was the quiet one, the softest spoken. Of these innately gentle men, he was the gentlest. Linsey wondered what great hurt or what cruelty in his young life had made him so acutely aware of the hurts of others.

"Don't mind Jackson," the youngest Cade said. "He's happiest when he's teasing some sweet young thing or baiting us."

Jefferson stood with one foot resting on the low garden wall. His left hand lay on his bent knee, with his right he clasped Cade's shoulder. The sight of her son reminded Linsey that all of this, and all she must endure in the near future, was for Cade. She looked from her son to Jefferson again, and the compassion in the dark-blue gaze and the encouraging smile of this most sensitive of the Cades soothed her.

The smile became a grin, changing his features, lighting his eyes. Linsey realized Jefferson was astonishingly handsome. Given his looks and the hint of tragic secrets in his laughter, he was surely lethal to the female population of Belle Terre and the surrounding territory. What woman with eyes and a heart wouldn't wish she could hold him and kiss the hurt to make it better?

Except, Linsey remembered, long ago in speaking of his brothers, Lincoln had called Jefferson the loner. He loved his brothers fiercely, even joined in some of the brotherly hell-raising. Not one Cade doubted he would walk through fire and give his life for them. Yet there was a part of Jefferson that couldn't fit. A part he held aloof.

In Lucky's tales to Cade, the youngest of the disparate brothers, the one he fondly called Jeffie became the young Daniel Boone of the lowcountry. A man of action who would rather hunt and fish and explore the swamps, studying creatures he would paint later. He could be gracious, debonair, and dynamic when the occasion arose, but it was the solitary things that consumed him.

Jefferson was a handsome, fascinating enigma. Linsey wondered how many belles of Belle Terre had lost themselves in those magnificent blue eyes, only to be disappointed when he wasn't interested. Poor girls. Poor Jeffie, to have so much, yet feel he deserved nothing.

In this common bond, she addressed the solitary Cade. "A home is the reflection of its surroundings. What you've restored and planned will make it a better place for Cade. A place he can be proud of and cherish as Lucky cherished it. For that I can never thank you enough."

When she had begun these speeches, her manner and voice were stilted. Before she finished, she'd spoken from her heart, addressing each honestly but differently. For despite their bond as brothers, beyond the honor and integrity they shared, no one would mistake them for replications of each other.

That each could overwhelm with a look or a word was inarguable. That together they could brawl and apart they could love with the best, she didn't question. That they were too impressive, too handsome, too everything, Linsey had witnessed.

But when she would have forgotten they were still truly just men, it was Lincoln who had reminded her.

*They're Cades...*
*Mortal men...*
*My brothers...*
*Never presume to judge.*

Her command performance behind her, the broken rhythm of Lincoln's words branded her memory. From it Linsey drew courage. A lift of her head, a signaling pressure on Lincoln's arm, and she was ready to descend the steps of the Stuart farm. Ready to move among these men to whom she owed so much. Among whom, the Cades willing, she would raise her son.

"Shall we?" Responding to the change in her, Lincoln folded his free hand over hers. His fingers touched the chafed skin of her knuckles, made an angrier red by the white of the gauze binding her palm. A guttural note sounded in his throat as he stroked the roughened flesh one last time, before letting his arm fall at his side.

Linsey looked up at him, trying to fathom this shift in his mood. But his face was too well schooled to reveal his feelings. Impossible as it seemed, after little personal contact she understood Adams, Jackson, and Jefferson better than this man who had been her friend.

"Lincoln, is something wrong?" she asked on impulse.

His name and the distress in her voice drew him from his thoughts. Looking down at the changes in the face he remembered so well, he murmured, "Nothing's wrong, Linsey. Nothing except you've worked too hard for too long. Nothing except..." A muscle rippled in his jaw as he searched for the right words.

Linsey waited, not daring to breathe. His brothers and Eden and Cade were waiting, too. It didn't matter. Nothing mattered but Lincoln and what he might say.

The moment stretched between them. A board creaked in protest of some subtle shift of the house. A whippoorwill sang too soon of evening. Noelle laughed, the sweet note breaking even the darkest mood.

With a slow tilt of his head, as if the strange interlude hadn't been, Lincoln smiled only for her. ''It isn't important. At least it won't be soon.''

Drawing her arm close, he let her feel the beat of his heart, the heat of his body, the steady rise and fall of his breathing and, perhaps, the need he'd hidden for weeks. This day marked the initiation of a plan he hoped would culminate in what was best for all. For Linsey, for himself. For Cade.

''We have this day. A celebration of an end and a beginning. Let's enjoy it.'' His smile warmed his eyes. ''Shall we join the others, Linsey, and let the celebration commence?''

He was speaking in riddles, but so gently any obscure purpose wasn't important to her. For, when he smiled at her as he smiled now, she would go with him wherever he asked. Into the midst of his brothers. To heaven. To hell. Anywhere.

''Yes.'' Her voice wavered, but as she clasped his arm, there was strength and the first of hope in her touch. ''It's time.''

''Then,'' he said softly, ''we begin.''

Her foot touching the first step served as a sign the festivities had been set in motion, for both Jackson and Jefferson were waiting at the last. Each vying in Jackson's formal phrasing, ''for the honor of escorting the lady of the manor to the repast awaiting her within the cool shade of the oaks.''

While each offered his arm with Southern chivalry, in keeping with this courtly little speech, Lincoln swept Linsey past them. In a drawl that didn't sound quite like a tease, he said, "Sorry. You have to find your own lady. This one is mine."

When they passed near Cade, still standing as Jefferson left him, his face alight with laughter, a sun darkened, brawny hand extended to him. Waiting until small fingers twined with his, Lincoln amended, "My lady and Cade's."

Her son's name on his father's lips sent first a frisson of pleasure, then apprehension through Linsey. The first was short-lived as the second stunned her, shaking her fledgling confidence as a gale would a reed, leaving her to wonder how this charade would end. How, when, by whom.

As she'd worked alone in the house these last days, her mind filled with the past as much as the present, there was never any doubt who should end the waiting game. She knew it was she who should speak. Yet the right moment, a quiet and private occasion, had never presented itself. Now time was running short.

Soon his brothers would be gone. Then there would be only Lincoln and Cade and Linsey. At least until his protracted sabbatical from his veterinary practice ended. She would tell him then. Before that last day. Perhaps while Cade explored the creek, too deep in thought and too excited by his discoveries to overhear. Better still, when he chased rabbits with Brownie, ranging far from the sound of their voices.

It would seem strange to tell Lincoln what he surely knew. But, yes, she would tell him soon. The decision made at last, Linsey felt as if the heaviest burden of her life had been lifted. Dread was never the equal of guilt.

Her smile was only a little strained as Cade slipped free of Lincoln's grasp, dancing ahead a step or two, leading the way. Once she even managed a chuckle, then a very real gasp of delight when he turned and gestured with a gleeful, "Look, Mom, your surprise. Isn't it swell?"

*Swell* was Cade's word describing the epitome of wonderful and amazing, and any number of exciting discoveries. The shady nook where he and Lincoln had led her was certainly a bit of each and more. "My goodness, tiger, I would say it's swell, indeed."

Stepping away from Lincoln, she moved closer to their son. The place that had been the dining area of various work crews had been transformed. Where sawhorses and boards covered by oilcloth had been, sat a smaller table laid with linen and silver and crystal, along with an array of foods that would never have come from the kitchen of Miss Corey. Though appetizing, hers were the sturdy and filling, no-nonsense meals of the working man.

This smaller table was one of celebration, the food exotic and appealing. Fare for the gourmet, rather than the gourmand. The aroma wafting from pretty dishes was intoxicating.

Linsey wasn't certain if it was the sight and smell of the food, or that she hadn't eaten all day, but she was ravenous. Which would shock each of the Cades. At one time or another, Lincoln, Adams, Jackson, and even Jefferson had scolded her when she skipped or skimped over one of Miss Corey's hearty meals. Neither understood that when she was tense or worried or tired, the first casualty of either was her appetite.

"Madame, may I seat you and serve a plate for you?" Linsey looked up, then up again. A giant stood waiting solicitously at her shoulder. A giant dressed in an impeccable white dinner jacket, who moved like a silent wind, had the look of a Pacific Islander, and spoke perfect, barely accented English.

"Cullen." Lincoln clasped hands with the golden-skinned, dark-haired Goliath and spoke fondly. "I should have known you wouldn't be far away with Eden and Noelle in attendance."

Cullen grinned and made a little bow. "I am wrapped firmly around the little fingers."

"Like the rest of the world. The Cades included." Lincoln turned to Linsey. Taking her hand in his again, he smiled down at her in a way he'd never smiled before. "Darling, meet Cullen, Eden's friend, confidant, major-domo, and nursemaid."

Linsey pretended she understood. But Lincoln had called her darling as if it were the most natural thing. After the uncommon endearment which, though she couldn't explain why, was more unsettling than his casual "love," or the teasing "sweetheart," she hadn't comprehended a word he said. Trying to reorganize her scrambled brains, she remembered the giant's name was Cullen only because she'd heard it before Lincoln turned to her, to look at her as if she were the center of his universe.

"I think nursemaid should head the list." Jackson stood a pace behind them. "And a damned good one he is, too."

"At least as good as Jackson," Jefferson chimed in, his face solemn, but his beautiful eyes wonderfully alive with laughter. "Talk about wrapped around a finger. Our little girl has reeled old Jackson in hook, line, and sinker. He may even abandon the wallflower line when our girl attends her first dance."

"Leave it to our swamp scout to talk in fishing terms," Jackson groused, but with a chuckle. "Don't think Lincoln isn't one bit less smitten than the rest of us, Linsey, love."

Lincoln laughed, making no attempt to deny that he was mad about little Noelle. Instead he looked down at Cade, wrapped a palm around a small, sturdy shoulder and drew the boy close. "Now we have another one. A little older, a bit less dainty, but no less the conqueror. I heard you all today, arguing over who would have Cade as his helper because he's such good company."

Glancing at Cade, finding a look of awe on the young face, Lincoln winked and tugged his favorite Stetson to the tip of a sunburned nose. "Right, tiger?"

"Right." The Stetson was pushed back by the pad of Cade's thumb. A move Linsey had seen Lincoln make countless times in the past weeks. A boy emulating the man he could only see through the eyes of love and admiration.

Linsey fought back a surge of emotion. She managed a laugh when Cade crossed his arms over his chest, widened his stance as much as Lincoln's boots would allow and announced to the crowd, "Adams says he likes to be with me 'cause I ask good questions."

"Well, now, I don't think anyone would argue with that." Surprising Cade, Jefferson scooped him up and set him on his shoulders. "How about we go to the stream and wash some of that Stuart farm grunge off your hands while the others serve their plates. When we come back, we'll eat all that's left."

"What's grunge? Why do you wear a string of blue rocks in your hair? Can I really eat all of the pie that looks like shaving cream?" Cade was grinning as if Jefferson's shoulders were a throne and he a prince as they jogged away to the stream.

Linsey didn't hear Jefferson's answer, for Eden took that opportunity to speak. "It's true. They have taken to the boy. Adams regales Cullen and me with tales of Cade each night."

Linsey turned to the woman she'd met only once before. In the first days of her time on the Stuart farm, Eden had visited, introducing herself and offering to help in any way she could. Promising she wouldn't intrude, but that she would never be more than a call away, she'd left the farm, keeping her word.

Linsey hadn't called, of course, for while the Cades were about, she had only to think of a need, or voice a concern, and either would be resolved. She hadn't needed Eden, until today. For the moral support, for the comfort simply having a woman who knew the Cades so well lent her.

"I'm glad you could come today, Eden. This is a bit…"

As Linsey hesitated, her voice drifting away, Eden laughed. "I know how you feel. I think the word is overwhelming. The Cades have a way of doing that to a woman without trying.''

''A way of doing what?'' Lincoln turned from bantering with Adams and Jackson in time to hear the comment.

''Overwhelm, Lincoln.'' Eden tapped his cheek fondly. ''You Cades have a way of overwhelming the rest of the world.''

''Ha!'' He looped an arm around Linsey, drew her before him, then folded both arms at her waist. ''Tell that to this one. Or Noelle. I suspect they're both significantly underwhelmed by us. Right, love?''

This time the soft, tender tone of his endearment registered only a millisecond before she felt the soft touch of his lips and the warmth of his breath at her temple. Even as her heart lurched, she tried to tell herself it meant nothing, that it was part of some game he played for his brothers. Maybe for Cade. That he could be so convincing was proof of the charisma of the Cades. Of all the Cades. Jackson had called her ''love'' and looked at her as if he truly cared about her, even as he teased wickedly.

This shared magnetism should have seemed strange in that each of the Cades had separate mothers and each was his mother's son with little of their father. But in only a brief time it was easy to see that in their hearts they were very much the same. Lucky had spoken of this phenomenon in tales he told Cade of his adventures with the four brothers, and especially with Lincoln.

Linsey had discovered the truth of it in the weeks these astonishingly generous men made the restoration of a home for Lucky Stuart's widow their first priority. As assiduously as she'd avoided them in her daily routine, the truth was ever there to be discovered and rediscovered in acts of caring and generosity. It was here today in their welcoming smiles.

And, if she could believe it, in Lincoln's tender words and in his kiss.

A game. It had to be a game. But for now she wouldn't call his hand. Not before she saw where he was going with it.

"Underwhelmed?" With a finger slowly she stroked the length of his hand from fingertip to wrist as it lay against her. Deciding two could play his game, whatever it might be, she murmured, "By a Cade? Any Cade? Never."

Eden laughed and clasped Adams's free hand in hers. "I would say you've met your match, Lincoln Cade."

Lincoln didn't miss a beat as he replied, "I hope so, for in time I plan to ask this lady—"

"Lincoln." Jefferson's voice was steady, but something in it sent fear spiraling through Linsey. Before she turned, and even though it was Lincoln's name he called as a vacuum closed around her shutting out everything and everyone, she knew this was about Cade. But nothing prepared her for what she saw.

Blood. The world and Jefferson were red with it.

Red.

With Cade's blood.

# Six

The smell assaulted her. Drifting like fog, it permeated every space, tainted every breath. Filling her lungs, her memory, it clawed at her until it took all her strength not to scream.

Clinging to fraying control, Linsey stared at her hands gripped so tightly her fingers were growing numb. And even her palm, with the cut redressed at Lincoln's insistence in gauze so white it was an eye-straining blur beneath unforgiving lights.

But she couldn't turn away. She couldn't look up, she didn't want to see. She didn't want to remember.

Through the course of Lucky's illness she'd learned to dread the shadowless, sterile halls of hospitals. Those austere institutions of hope and healing, with clean, medicinal smells sullied by the underlying stench of illness, of injury. Of death.

She didn't want to remember, but she couldn't forget Lucky's broken body and the bloody odor sifting past massive doors that locked her away from him. Leaving her more alone than she'd ever been, with the miasma of death no medicine could overpower.

She couldn't forget, but in time she'd learned to banish it to the back of her mind as the pain of his death and her grief, if not her guilt, began to diminish. Now the unthinkable had happened. It was Cade who lay behind another fortress of doors. The reek of blood that filled her every breath was his.

Frozen in fear, tangled in memories, and praying life wasn't repeating itself, she listened without hearing, waiting for someone to come to her. Someone with news of her son.

Hushed footsteps padded past. Each cadence unfamiliar, each different. Some scuffed, some marched, another raced, in urgency. None faltered at the door of the waiting room that was her prison. No matter that her heart quickened with hope, with dread, with fear, none slowed for longer than a pitying glance.

By ever-increasing experience, Linsey had discovered that "no news is good news" wasn't a cliché in times of fear and dread. It was, instead, cruelty. Unintentional, unavoidable, perhaps or certainly, but cruelty still.

So she listened. She waited. She prayed.

Finally, unable to bear the void of not knowing, she lifted her head to stare down the long, brutally lit hall. The doors she wanted to throw herself against, to beg, to plead, to demand to be let in, were closed so solidly she feared they might never open. Yet, staring at it, she willed them to swing wide and give back her small, delightful son, whole and uninjured.

She stared so long her eyes began to ache, but she dared not blink. For with so much as the flicker of an eye, the image of Cade would be there. But not Cade as she willed him to be.

Like the negative of a black-and-white photograph, the

imprint of her son in Jefferson's arms, a slashed and torn boot still embedded in the flesh of his splinted leg was etched on the back of her eyelids. In bleak tones of black, in somber shades of white and gray, and red with blood, it lay in wait for her. Cade's blood covering more of Jefferson than himself, streaking like scarlet lightning through her mind.

Dear God! She couldn't shut her eyes. Couldn't let herself see. Couldn't let herself think.

"Linsey."

The pleasing scent of cedar, fresh air and soap engulfed her. But even that was no match for memories and fear.

"Linsey, darling, he's in good hands." The leather sofa dipped as Lincoln came to sit by her. His hand covered hers. The warmth of his clasp, the strength should have comforted her. But Linsey was beyond comfort. Beyond anything but terror.

"Drink this." He held a cup of dark tea laced with lemon.

As chaotic as her thoughts had been, on another level she'd been acutely aware of Lincoln. Aware that it was he who took Cade from Jefferson, holding the unconscious child throughout the nightmare journey. He who relinquished his precious burden into skillful hands, then watched over her as carefully while a nurse redressed a wound Linsey had forgotten. Throughout the ordeal he'd left her for only seconds. And yet the tea.

"I'm not a magician. Eden sent this," he answered the question in her look. "Thinking you might like something other than soft drinks or the tar that masquerades as coffee in waiting rooms, she charmed the head dietitian out of a pot of a private stash the lady keeps for herself. Don't ask me how Eden knew that little tidbit, but she did." He offered the cup again. "For you."

When she didn't respond, setting the cup aside, he opened her fingers and drew her cold hands apart. Placing the cup between them, then folding his own large, strong hands over hers, he pleaded, "Try one sip. Only one. Then, if you can't drink it, just hold it. Let it warm you a little."

Obediently she took one sip, her eyes downcast. More than warming her, the tea served as a reminder. She'd been so caught up in her own fears she'd forgotten that this time she wasn't alone. This time there were others to care. Others to share her vigil.

"Vigil." For Linsey it was a word without hope. When she lifted her gaze again to Lincoln's her eyes were hollow, her lips pale and thin as she searched his face for answers she feared she hadn't been given. "Is that what this is? A vigil?"

"No, love." Taking the tea from her and setting it aside, careful of her injured palm, Lincoln took her hands in his. Raising first one, then the other to his lips, he brushed a kiss over chafed knuckles and smiled. A concerned but not a frightened smile. It was heartbreaking to see her like this, desolate, helpless, afraid.

It hurt to know that she'd suffered the long agony of waiting before. It hurt more that she'd endured it alone, with no one to whom she could turn. No one who cared as she cared.

Not this time or ever again, Lincoln vowed, beginning to understand more of this woman. Of her choices and their reason. Of her brave life and the life she'd given her son. And his.

*His son.*

The words sliced through him like a knife in the heart. Yes, Cade was his. He'd known it from the moment he'd watched the boy run into his mother's arms to dance on the Stuart porch in the light of a setting sun. He would have known anywhere, anytime. Only a blind man wouldn't know.

His brothers knew. The knowledge was there in their eyes when they looked at Cade. But none spoke of it. And as he promised Linsey, none of them presumed to judge what they didn't understand. Even Jackson had bided his time, and his tongue, waiting as Adams and Jefferson waited, for him.

A wait of caution Lincoln Cade's pragmatic, stubborn streak wouldn't admit was worse than stupid. Until now.

Whatever the past. Whatever Linsey's reason, or his guilt, his concern was Cade. And the woman by his side.

"This isn't Lucky all over again, Linsey." He was more than a little apprehensive that he might make everything worse rather than better. Yet, when he looked at her, small and fragile, he had to try. "This is Cade. His injury is serious, not life threatening. He's strong, he's young, he has you. That puts the odds in his favor. Especially having you."

Linsey's fingers flexed in his clasp. Her gaze searching deeply into his. "Do you really mean that?"

"I really mean it. With no qualifications."

"But..."

"But nothing, Linsey. Nothing. All we need to think about now is getting Cade well." Leaning back in his seat, he kept her uninjured hand in his. "I spoke with a nurse just now.

"Actually," he grinned, and lifted a heavy shoulder, "I accosted her. When she realized I wasn't going away until I got what I wanted, she called for a progress report on Cade."

Though he wouldn't have thought it possible, Linsey paled even more. Her eyes were like lasers searching his face with fearful hope. "All she could tell me is that surgery went well and we should be hearing something definitive within a half hour.

"By then Adams and Eden will be back from the cafeteria. Jackson should have finished checking his horses and will bring Jefferson a change of clothes." With the back of his free hand he stroked her cheek, wishing he could put color back in the smooth curve. Letting his knuckles trail to the corner of her mouth, he settled for a touch, rather than the kiss he longed for.

"Jefferson?" Linsey tensed as Lincoln's hand drifted from her. Mesmerized by his caress, the import of his words registered slowly. "Jefferson's still here? He's been here the whole time and I haven't seen him?"

Lincoln wondered at this unexpected intensity and its meaning. "Where else would he be, Linsey? Where would any of us be, but here? Jackson wouldn't have left even for a while if he weren't shorthanded at his stables at River Trace."

"Where is Jefferson?" Disengaging her hand from Lincoln's, for the first time in over an hour, Linsey stood, unconsciously intending to pace. An old habit from the times Lucky's hospitalizations stretched into interminable, unbearable loneliness. She stared around the comfortable waiting room, realizing there was nowhere to walk but the short distance to a private elevator. Except down the hall toward the doors that sealed Cade away from her.

Cade. He was here to be treated in Belle Terre Trauma Center because of Jefferson.

Concerned for Jefferson, beginning to think of the fear and grief of someone other than herself, she spun around to find that Lincoln had stood, as well. In an instinctive thought, she realized she'd expected he would. That much about him hadn't changed since the days of the past. A courtesy ingrained in him. One that never altered. No matter the time, place, or the woman.

Laying a hand on the left side of his chest, she let her fingertips rest briefly against him before curling them into her palm. Even then she could feel the beat of his heart. Strong and steady, like the man he'd become. She needed to unburden herself, to bring truth to reality. But it would be unfair to open a festering wound out of weakness and fear.

This day had hurt enough people already. Hurting another could wait.

She moved away from Lincoln. He made no effort to touch her or draw her back. For that she was grateful. Sympathy would be her undoing. Gathering hard-won strength, she asked, "Where is Jefferson? I'd like to see him."

Lincoln was surprised but encouraged by the change in her. He didn't question its cause. "A high school classmate of his is a resident here. Jeffie mooched a shower, a pair of scrubs, and a place to hide out until Jackson gets back with a change of clothing." Hesitating, he added, "And until we get word on Cade."

"A place to stay, until we hear about Cade? But why?" Breaking off her questions, Linsey came to grips with the truth of how unaware she'd been of how profoundly the accident affected those who cared about Cade. How oblivious she'd been of people who had been kind to both mother and son.

Though it hardly penetrated at the time, she remembered that Adams and Eden and Jackson had never left her side until Jackson was forced to leave to see to his stock. Eden chose that same time to slip away to call Cullen, who had stepped in, taking charge of Noelle and anything else needing attention. Adams seized the opportunity after Eden's call to whisk her away to the cafeteria for the dinner no one had eaten.

Even then, Eden had thought of Linsey. Realizing she couldn't eat under stress, sending tea instead.

"And Jefferson staying away, but near, because he felt the sight of him would hurt." In her wondering and inhibited wandering, she'd turn away from Lincoln. Now she turned back. "Call him, please. Tell him I'd like to see him."

Lincoln was doubtful. "I'm not sure this is a good time."

"Please. There's no better time."

Raking his fingers through his hair, already disheveled

from countless other such forays during the hours of waiting, Lincoln yielded reluctantly. "If you're sure."

"I've never been more positive."

"Then I won't be but a minute." He hesitated. "If you need me, I'll be at the in-house phones around the corner."

"Thank you." Linsey's smile was weak but real. The numb, unthinking paralysis of fear had given way to reason and control. This was Cade, not Lucky. Cade who was young and strong and in the best of hands.

As if this new awareness made time pass more swiftly, sooner than she thought possible Lincoln was back by her side. As he had been from the beginning, lending strength with his silent support. In a smooth, noiseless glide, the private elevator opened. Jefferson stepped out. Instead of scrubs, he wore jeans that were too big and a shirt that was snug at the shoulders. His boots had been scrubbed clean and bore no mark of Cade's blood.

His face was composed, but his wonderful eyes held a deep sadness when his gaze met Linsey's. Linsey didn't know what deep hurtful guilt Jefferson Cade carried in his heart. But her Cade shouldn't be another.

Going to him, taking his callused hands in hers, she looked up at him. "Thank you."

"No…"

"Yes," Linsey insisted before he could abjure more. "If it weren't for you, Cade could have drowned in the stream when he fainted. Or bled to death."

"Maybe." Jefferson was unable to keep her gaze. "But if I'd seen the trap, he wouldn't be here."

Linsey lifted an incredulous brow. "Then it's common in South Carolina to have bear traps set in streams?"

"Of course not." Jefferson's anger replaced guilt. "I've found traps like these in the swamp. Set, then forgotten or abandoned to inflict whatever damage they might. I can't imagine what fool could have set it on Stuart land. Or why in the underbrush at the edge of the stream."

"I doubt we'll ever know, Jeffie." Lincoln stood by Linsey. "We know deer come to drink. It could've been left by a poacher who dared not risk a gunshot. Or a neighboring farmer after a fox raiding henhouses."

"Name me one that close, or that stupid," Jefferson challenged his brother. "What fool in his right mind would do this? The trap was overkill, at the least."

"And who would think to look for something this stupid and unheard of?" Linsey asked quietly, making her point again.

"Obviously, I didn't." Jefferson was not to be relieved of his guilt so easily.

"You did all the right things," Linsey countered. "Things I couldn't have done. In the first place, I wouldn't have had the strength to open the trap. In the second place—" Breaking off, with a shake of her head, she said, "If I could, I would undo all that happened today. Since I can't, I'm thankful for the single blessing in it—that you were with Cade."

Stepping forward, with her heart in her eyes, she wrapped her arms around this sad young man. Holding him, wishing for better words, she whispered, "Thank you, Jefferson Cade, for your quick thinking, for all you did for my son. For the man you are."

For a moment after Linsey released Jefferson and stepped away, Lincoln said nothing. Then he clasped his brother's shoulder. "I doubt anyone could say it better than Linsey. And I think you know she speaks for all of us. There isn't one among us who hasn't come to love Cade." Lincoln's voice roughened with emotion. "It's true, if there is any luck in this situation, it is that you were there. You have my gratitude for that, too, Jeffie."

"Hear! Hear!" Jackson stood a pace behind them. Adams and Eden by his side. "My thoughts exactly, and I would have told him so myself if I thought he would listen."

"So would we all." Going to Jefferson, Eden rose on tiptoes to kiss his cheek. "You've served as well as guardian angel for Cade as you have as godfather for Noelle."

Turning to Linsey, her smile faded to concern. "Is there any news?"

On cue, massive doors at the end of the hall swished open, then closed behind a tall man swathed in green from head to toe. As he walked, footsteps muted by incongruous running shoes, he slipped a mask from his face and a cloth cap from his head. Hair the color of dark honey and streaked with silver fell over his forehead and brushed the nape of his neck. Eyes a shade paler than his hair swept over those who waited, frozen and unmoving, as they'd been when the doors opened for him.

A swift and silent acknowledgment of each of the Cades, then his golden gaze settled on Linsey. "Mrs. Stuart." His voice was low and gentle and seemed to come from a deep well of compassion. "I'm Davis Cooper. Best known as Cooper or Coop to my friends."

Linsey took the hand he offered, then went with him as he led her to a sofa. "First," he said as he sat by her, "Cade's leg is going to be fine. You can put your mind to ease on that." The solemn lines of his face softened as his glance touched on each of the Cades again, in turn. "The fortune in this was where it happened, who was there, and what was done.

"And, to toot my own horn, the Center." One corner of his mouth tilted in the smallest suggestion of a smile. "There's good news and not so good. The good is it was a simple fracture. The bad news is the wound is the greatest complication.

"That would be obvious to someone with your background in park service." Davis Cooper continued not so solemnly, "Tooting the horn again, what might not be so readily apparent is that despite the Center's small size, its reputation and integrity command astute medical minds and extraordinarily skilled practitioners. Many of whom are part of the team treating Cade.''

Linsey was a stranger here. She would have expected her son to be no more than a name and number. One more damaged body to repair. ''Why would Cade Stuart merit such care?''

The lift at the corner of Cooper's mouth grew into a legitimate smile. ''The fact that he's here. That he needs us. There's no other criteria. Even a call from a man the caliber of Lincoln Cade informing that a boy who is his namesake was being brought in would be no spur toward care more special than your son is receiving.

''Belle Terre Trauma Center offers one service to all, our best.'' A frown crossed the strong classical features of Davis Cooper. ''There is one unique element about Cade that gives cause for extra measures.''

Linsey tensed. The hiss of a harshly indrawn breath was the only sound she made as she waited for this stranger who held her child's life in his hands to say what he must.

''Given the time it took Jefferson to prize the trap open, Cade lost more blood than we like to see, but not enough to be critical. Under ordinary circumstances we would simply send him home with detailed instructions and a warning to take it easy.''

''These aren't ordinary circumstances, are they, Coop?'' Lincoln had come to stand behind Linsey. She'd focused so exclusively on Davis Cooper, for once she hadn't been aware of the pleasing scent that always announced his presence.

Cooper shrugged in a gesture of regret. ''Being clawed by a trap that's been God knows where, caught only God knows what, can hardly be called ordinary. Who knows how long the blasted thing lay there in the tall weeds by the creek? Or how long in the water? A month? A week? A day?''

''You're concerned about infection.'' Lincoln had seen

it with his four-legged patients. He knew traps, how insidious and invasive the resulting infections could be. He knew they could be fatal. Especially with one whose resistance and resilience was hampered by complications.

Cooper looked up at Lincoln. "We've done everything in our power to see that doesn't happen."

"*But* infections in cases like Cade's are unpredictable. At times nothing is enough," Lincoln finished for him. At Linsey's stifled moan, he curled a palm around her shoulder, offering the encouragement he could.

"There is one more thing we can add to our arsenal to slant the odds in Cade's favor," Cooper suggested. "A transfusion, to build him up quicker. To give him more strength and resilience to fight infection. Should it occur."

Now it was Lincoln who frowned. "I don't see the problem. Unless there's some ethical objection." Lincoln leaned down. When he was eye level with Linsey, his gaze probed her frantic countenance. Though the idea didn't fit the woman he'd known, he recognized that the interim of so many years since he'd seen her and truly known her could have wrought equally as many changes. Making his words a question rather than a doubtful speculation, he asked, "Would you object, Linsey?"

"Of course not." Any other time she would have been upset, angry that Lincoln would question that she might deny her son any weapon in this battle. But for now her strength mustn't be squandered on anger. Her focus must be Cade and Cade's needs. Turning to Cooper, in a tone hardly more than a whisper, she pleaded, "Do everything you can for him. Anything. Please."

Her voice broke. The despair she'd fought for so long became reality. "Cade's all I have."

"We'll do everything in our power." Cooper studied her lovely, harried face, adding reluctantly, "But it isn't quite that simple."

Linsey was acutely aware of Lincoln's hand lying on her shoulder and that he was as intent on Cooper's judgment as she admitted, "I know."

"Then you're aware your son's blood type is quite rare?" Cooper didn't wait for an answer. One glance and he didn't need one. "And therein lies our second problem. Belle Terre is a small, affluent city. In this case, it's size that works against us. We have generous donors, but few of Cade's type."

Cooper's voice softened as if he might diminish a blow. "In an extraordinary coincidence and appalling timing, an accident on the Interstate depleted much of our blood supply. We've sent out a call to our regular donors, but I was hoping for someone closer to the boy."

The handsome features of the physician contorted into regret as Linsey flinched and grew even paler. Drawing a long resigned breath, his lips tightened in resignation. "You and Cade don't share the same blood type, do you, Mrs. Stuart?"

Though not truly a question, Linsey whispered, "No."

"Take mine," Lincoln said quietly.

Cooper looked up, and for the first time a real smile eased the concern on his face.

"It is the same, isn't it, Coop?"

For a moment Cooper said nothing. Then, as if his faith in men had been vindicated, his smile grew and brightened. If Linsey had been aware of anything or anyone but Lincoln, she would have seen that, like Jefferson's, that particular smile made a pleasantly attractive man extraordinary.

But Linsey didn't see, and all she heard was Davis Cooper replying, "I hoped you'd volunteer."

"Did you think for one second I wouldn't?" When he'd first spoken, Lincoln had moved a step back from Linsey.

As she made a half turn to stare at him, Linsey was not sure what she might see, or even what she wanted to see in his face. In his eyes. But Lincoln wasn't looking at her. Instead he concentrated on unbuttoning the starched cuffs of his shirt and rolling back the sleeves. A process that seemed to take forever.

"Lincoln?" she said, her voice rising in the quavering lilt of a question she hadn't dared ask.

"Shh," he murmured as he looked up from his finished task to stroke the line of her cheek with the tips of his fingers. "Everything's going to be all right. Everything and everyone. We'll work this out for Cade. But before we can look to the future, we have to deal with the present.

"The present is here, this minute, in this hospital. And, for the first time in his life, Cade needs me."

With a look entrusting Linsey to his brothers' care, he spoke gently to her. "Adams and Jackson and Jefferson will be here. And Eden. If you need anything, ask, and whatever you want will be done."

Over his shoulder he spoke to Cooper, who stood now. "How soon should we do this?"

"The sooner, the better for Cade."

Lincoln nodded his head in acknowledgment, but never looked away from Linsey. "Then let's do better." His fingers trailed again over the soft skin of her cheek. "I won't be long. When this is over, we'll take Cade home. Together."

*Cade.*

Lincoln had called his name. Within the past few hours he'd said it time and again. But never quite like this. Linsey couldn't speak. She couldn't find the words that would say enough of her gratitude. Enough of love.

Instead she only stared at him. At Lincoln. Pale, her eyes shining with all she couldn't speak, she smiled. When Lincoln smiled in return and bent to brush her mouth with his, her lips trembled, and hope was born in her heart.

He straightened. Standing tall above her, he held her gaze

for a long moment, then turned away. "Ready, Davis Cooper?"

"As ready as I'll ever be, Lincoln Cade."

"Then, let's do it."

Huddled on the sofa, Linsey watched as Lincoln walked the long hall side by side with Cooper. She watched as, together, they disappeared behind the fortress of forbidding doors.

The wait had begun again. But for the first time in longer than she could remember, Linsey didn't feel so lost, so alone.

*We'll take Cade home. Together.*

"Home," she whispered, as if saying the words aloud would break some magic spell. "Together."

# Seven

"Morning, tiger."

Linsey turned from the window overlooking a river park adjacent to Belle Terre Trauma Center. A glance at Cade proved the boy was, indeed, awake and smiling at Lincoln, who stood in the doorway, a book and a beribboned package in his hands.

"Lincoln!" Despite the metal brace holding his leg and weighing him down, Cade struggled to pull himself erect. As Linsey moved to help, he managed a weak smile, but his attention was drawn immediately back to Lincoln. "Mom said you might be too busy to come by today. 'Specially after you spent so much time at the farm, then the other days here at the hospital."

"Not a chance." Lincoln crossed to stand by Linsey at Cade's bedside. "I'm still a vet at leisure. To tell the truth, all I had to do today was check on my dad and speak with Jesse Lee about some matters at Belle Reve. Even if there had been more to do, I'd have time for my shotgun rider."

Cade's smile drooped. A frown furrowed his forehead. "Guess it'll be a long time before I ride shotgun on the mower again. And the new colt Mr. Jesse showed me will prob'ly be growed up before I can see him some more."

Looking to Linsey, Cade explained, "Mr. Jesse is foreman at the plantation, and a real live cowboy from Ari...Ari..."

"Arizona," Lincoln supplied.

"Yep," Cade agreed. "A cowboy and a expert on horses. 'Cept he calls them *hosses*. Guess it'll prob'ly be a long time before I see him again, too."

"Maybe not as long as you think." Laying the book and package aside, Lincoln looked at Linsey. The fleeting frown that marred his features was quickly abandoned. If she saw his concern, she would deny the toll Cade's accident had taken.

Lincoln had been worried, fearing this ordeal would be the last burden her exhausted mind and body could withstand. At first, he'd pleaded that she take the room Eden offered, where Cullen and the staff of The Inn at River Walk could watch over her in the rare instant no hovering Cades were around. When she refused, he tried for Lady's Hall, the old mansion on the infamous Fancy Row. Mansions that once were the homes of the mistresses of plantation owners in Belle Terre's Old South, reclaimed, refurbished, and given to the hospital as lodgings for parents of sick and injured children.

It hadn't surprised him when Linsey refused to leave Cade's bedside. "I can see Cade's well taken care of, but how are you?" One glance told him the truth he feared. "Have you slept?"

"Well enough." She indicated a massive lounge chair. "The Center sees to the comfort of worried parents. I slept as well the fifth night as the first."

"There's more to rest than bodily comfort." Cupping her cheek, with the pad of his thumb he skimmed over the darkened skin beneath her eye. Then moved to trace the curve of lips taut with accumulated fatigue and unrelieved strain. "So much more."

Such as a clear conscience and honesty. Linsey had wrestled with her own conscience and her lies by omission more keenly in the days since Cade's injury than ever before.

"It's okay if you kiss her," Cade chimed into her guilt-ridden thoughts. "I'm old enough to know that's what grown-ups like. Besides, Mom kisses good."

"Cade!" A rosy blush flooded Linsey's face with the color Lincoln had missed. Turning from his touch, she scolded the boy. "Wherever did you get such an idea?"

"I dunno." Cade lifted his shoulders in typical little-boy dismissal. But a gleam in his eyes warned Linsey she wasn't getting off that easily. "'Cept sometimes Lincoln looks at you like he's hurt or sad. Like now. And you do kiss good, and it does make it better. So I thought maybe..."

"I should kiss your mom?" A mischievous smile tilted Lincoln's lips, "Better yet, your mom should kiss me?"

"Yeah," Cade agreed. "That's exactly what I thought."

"You know what, tiger?" Lincoln let his gaze glide over the jutting angle of her jaw before it trailed down the graceful column of her throat to the hollow and the pulse that throbbed there. "I think you're right."

Startled by the tenderness in his voice and the caressing glide of his look, alarmed that it affected her more than it should, Linsey began to back away. Catching her uninjured hand, Lincoln drew her back, even closer. "Well, 'Mom'?" he said in a low drawl. "What do you think?"

"I think both of you could use a lesson in propriety. A hospital room isn't the place for such foolishness." Perhaps Lincoln wasn't touching her quite so tenderly, and perhaps this was all part of the game he seemed to be playing, but Linsey was still much too aware of her hand in his.

"Ahh, but who said we were fooling? This is serious

stuff. Right, Cade?'' Keeping her when she would have slipped away, Lincoln looked down at her. Though there was amusement in his voice, Linsey was captivated by a steady, gray gaze she couldn't fathom. Whatever she saw there could never be called amusement.

"Right. *Real* serious." The boy tried to keep a solemn face, but ended by dissolving into giggles.

Distracted by the wonderful sound she'd waited five long days to hear again, Linsey was caught off guard when Lincoln laced his fingers through hers, his thumb caressing the hollow of her palm. As her breath stuttered, he asked in a tone that suggested things Cade wouldn't understand, and she tried not to think about, "Well, 'Mom.' I'm waiting."

"First you gotta tell her where it hurts." Sighing Cade asked, "Heck, Lincoln, don't you know *anything?*"

"I guess I don't, tiger." Lincoln's thumb moved again in a secret caress over sensitive flesh. When she tried to draw away, he held her tighter. "I never had a mother, at least not for long. So I never learned the rules of this game."

"Like I didn't really have Lucky long 'cause he was sick so much?" The young voice quavered but was quickly controlled.

"Something like that. So you'll have to be patient while I learn the rules." Lincoln slanted Cade a solemn look. "You guarantee a kiss will make each hurt better?"

"Yes, sir." Cade's dark hair shone against the pristine pillow as he nodded, then shrugged. "Least it does for me."

"Lincoln," Linsey protested. "This is silly."

"Not to Cade and me." An exaggerated wink enlisted the boy's help. "Is it, tiger?"

"Not for me and you, Lincoln."

Lincoln's laughter reflected in his eyes. "See, 'Mom'?"

"I'm afraid I do." I see you're playing a game I don't understand, by your own rules, toward your own goals. The thought nagged at her. It would until she understood what he was doing and what he wanted. When she knew, what then?

"No, she doesn't, Lincoln," Cade insisted, drawing Linsey back into the game no one but she thought was strange. "'Less you're bleeding or something, Mom can't know till you show her."

"But there are so many places, where do we begin?" Lincoln pretended to think, then tapped his cheek. "How about here?"

"No." As she protested, Lincoln's thumb stroked across her palm in a tantalizing, remembered path. As before, she felt the impact of the tender gesture. "You can't be serious."

One dark brow lifted, in an innocent incredulity. "Sweetheart, this is as serious as Rudolph losing his red nose."

"Rudolph? In summer?" Cade burst into laughter. Though she tried to keep her composure, even Linsey smiled.

"You're hardly Rudolph." Inanely, for reasons she didn't understand, she added, "Anyway, as Cade said, it's summer."

"You're stalling, Linsey." Lincoln strove for a stern look and missed. It was the grin that won the day.

"Oh, all right. But I still say this is ridiculous." Lincoln had made Cade laugh as no one had in days. For that she could play their game and spare an innocent kiss.

Rising on tiptoe, quickly Linsey brushed her lips over the exact spot he'd touched. As quickly she retreated. But not so quickly the scent of him didn't curl through her in sweet trespass. Nor so soon that the feel of his skin beneath her lips didn't send out shock waves that were anything but innocent.

In desperate denial, she tried to move beyond the electric awareness that flowed between them. An awareness she knew was as apparent to Lincoln. A seductive consciousness born of need as intense as chain lightning streaking out of seething, churning heat, joining sky and earth on a sultry summer day.

As if by its own volition, her hand convulsed in his. But as before, Lincoln wouldn't allow Linsey her freedom.

"Not so fast, little coward." His voice was huskier now, softer, lazier. "There's more."

"Yeah, Mom." Oblivious of suggestive undercurrents, too young to understand the dangerous game his mother and his hero were playing, Cade was enjoying the repartee. Enough to forget the pain and the imprisoning brace. His face was less pinched in stress; a flush of color chased away the ivory tint of pallor. "Lincoln hurts lots of places. That means lots of kisses."

"Yeah, 'Mom,'" Lincoln echoed. "Lots."

"No." A pleading note, but she didn't resist.

"Give it up, sweetheart," Lincoln muttered before she could pursue her denial. "You aren't going to win, you know. Not when you're outnumbered by the men in your life. And Cade and I *are, and will always be,* the men in your life. Right, tiger?"

"Right." Cade was grinning a Cheshire Cat grin, pleased that Lincoln had called him a man.

Weariness she'd denied descended with a vengeance. She hadn't the strength to fight. "What do you want, Lincoln?"

"A kiss, sweetheart, to make it better. What else would I want?" He moved a step closer, his body touching hers.

"Where does it hurt?" Her own hurt glittered in her eyes.

"Here." Lincoln laid a closed fist over his heart. Linsey knew what he was saying, and understood its import. The threat of tears, denied so long, constricted her throat.

"Here," he repeated, moving his fist, opening it to touch his other cheek with his fingers. "But I'll settle for here."

Linsey wouldn't argue again. She couldn't. Steeling herself against the intoxicating feel of his skin beneath her kiss, she rose again on tiptoe to place her lips on the spot he indicated. To her dismay, no effort was strong enough to deny what she felt as, in the last instant Lincoln turned his head slightly, to take her lips with his. Nothing on earth could have prepared her for a kiss that seemed to go on forever.

A kiss plundering heart, mind and body, leaving no part of her unscathed by the need it kindled. A kiss blending anger and desperation and tender passion.

She didn't want to respond, didn't want him to know how vulnerable she still was and would always be. But even her own desperation couldn't stop her from responding to his. As he drew her hard against him, leaving no doubt this was more than a game, Linsey knew she was lost.

He'd kissed her before Cade's accident. Yet not like this. Then she'd been keenly aware of her every response. Now she didn't know that she trembled beneath his touch. Nor that she'd lifted her hands to hold him. Until she felt the slide of his hair through her questing fingers, she didn't realize how much she wished this kiss would never end. As her mouth opened to him, Linsey only knew that even if he hated her in the end, she couldn't deny him anything.

She swayed against him and would have clung for support. His hands clasping her shoulders, he put her away from him. When she flushed, confused, he smiled ruefully. "We have company."

Linsey turned, discovering that a small woman with silver-blond hair stood in the open doorway, her fisted hand still raised and resting against the door.

"I'm sorry, I knocked before I realized..." Pausing, she smiled contritely. "Forgive me, I didn't mean to intrude."

"No harm done, Haley," Lincoln said, as if he were interrupted in the midst of a kiss every day. "I'm glad you're here. Come meet my father's new neighbors."

Linsey was not a large woman, but as she moved from

the doorway, Lincoln's friend made her feel gigantic and unkempt. From the top of her sleek and shining hair to the tips of gleaming, black riding boots, this lovely stranger could barely be more than five feet tall—with the help of boots.

Though her first impression had been of exquisite elegance, Linsey suspected it was because the small woman would lend elegance to any circumstance—as she did with the clothing she wore, making sensible and utilitarian spectacular. A shirt of blue chambray, topped by a black leather vest was the perfect foil for her full breasts and small waist. Black jeans, cinched by a black belt, clinging modestly to narrow hips completed what Linsey believed was unheeded sartorial splendor.

When the woman called Haley turned to smile at Cade, Linsey saw that her long, thick hair was drawn back in a French braid banded with black circlets of elastic. No makeup was needed to correct an already perfect complexion. No khol or mascara enhanced eyes as dark-blue as midnight.

She was so beautiful, her smile so warm, Linsey felt her heart break as Lincoln went to Haley Garrett. And break a little more when he bent to kiss her lightly tanned cheek.

"Haley." Briefly taking her hand, he led her to the narrow bed with its bright, starched sheets. "Meet Cade Stuart. Cade, this is Dr. Garrett, a classmate of mine and an old friend."

"Ma'am." Cade ducked his head in shy greeting. Even a boy so young could be in awe of a woman who looked like an angel. "Do you really doctor animals and horses like Lincoln?"

"Hello, Cade, and yes, I doctor animals and horses like Lincoln." Haley Garrett offered her hand, affording him the courtesy she would an adult. "In fact, that's one reason I'm here. I made a barn call at Belle Reve early this morning. While I was there, Jesse Lee told me what a brave young man you are.''

''He did?'' Cade's eyes were alight with pleasure.

''That he did,'' Haley Garrett assured him. ''When I said I'd like to visit you, Jesse asked if I would deliver some messages for him. First is that Brownie likes it at Belle Reve, but he misses you. Second, the colt is good, but Jesse thinks the little fellow misses you, too. Nearly as much as Brownie.''

''Me? Sure Brownie misses me. We're buddies. But the colt, too?'' A hand flattened over a T-shirt-clad chest. ''For sure?''

''For sure.'' Haley Garrett crossed her heart solemnly. ''It happens that way with young colts sometimes. They bond fiercely with someone, perhaps by an instinct we humans don't understand. This colt chose you. So Jesse wanted me to ask if you would think of a name for the little fellow.''

''I can name him?'' Cade's shining gaze found Linsey. ''Did you hear that, Mom? I can name the colt.''

''That's wonderful, Cade.'' Linsey was pleased at the animation she saw in her son's face. ''Since he sounds like a special colt, you'll have to come up with a special name.''

''There's more,'' Haley said. ''When you lose the brace and both you and the colt are strong enough, Jesse thought you'd like to have a hand in its training.''

''I don't know how to train a horse.'' The boy fretted. ''What if I do it wrong?''

''Jesse will teach you as you teach the colt,'' Lincoln interjected into the conversation. ''There's no better teacher or trainer around except Jefferson, with Jackson and Merrie Alexandre, a lady you haven't met yet, not far behind.''

''Lucky said Jefferson comm...communed.'' Cade flashed a grin as he found the right word. ''That's it. He said Jefferson communed with animals.''

"I think he does," Lincoln agreed. "Especially with horses. But I think the same about Haley."

The lovely woman laughed in dismissal and turned, her brilliant smile finding Linsey. "Linsey Stuart, hello. I would have known you anywhere. As you heard in the midst of this foolishness, I'm Haley Garrett. What Lincoln neglected to say is that I'm his fairly new veterinary partner.

"I'm not quite up to Lincoln's assessment, but I do well with animals and kids. Which is fortunate, since at least one is involved in my chosen profession. I've been in Belle Terre a short while, and I haven't yet met Lincoln's brothers. But considering Jefferson's reputation with horses, I doubt I'm in his class."

Haley offered her hand. When Linsey took it, she was not startled by the callused strength of the smaller woman's clasp, for closer inspection proved the clothing the vet wore was truly utilitarian, the cut and faithful fit dictated by her work more than by fashion. That it suited her was incidental rather than contrived. What, Linsey wondered, *wouldn't* suit Haley Garrett?

"Thank you, Dr. Garrett. For what you've done for Cade. He was disappointed about missing out on all he'd planned for the summer. You've given him something to look forward to." Sincerely she added, "It has been my pleasure meeting you."

"Thank you, Linsey—if we can be just Linsey and Haley?" After a nod of agreement, Haley continued, as animated as before. "I'm so glad you're here at last. In the time he searched for you, I thought Lincoln would go mad with worry."

"Lincoln searched for me?" Startled, Linsey looked from Lincoln to Haley in question.

It was Lincoln who responded. "For more than a month."

Countless questions tumbled through Linsey's mind, but this wasn't the time to address them. "I didn't realize."

"And I didn't realize the time." A glance at a watch Haley drew from her vest pocket ended an awkward moment. "Lincoln, to explain my call at the plantation, Jesse wanted me to check one of his mares, not Jackson's. Actually, what he wanted was a second opinion to back up his own. It was nothing serious, and he's already taking care of it. Now I'm due at the office."

"You aren't going to River Trace?" Lincoln frowned. Jackson had a pregnant mare with a colt that might be too large. Until Cade's accident, he'd kept a weekly watch, hoping to save both. By now the visits should be scheduled almost daily.

"It seems that I'm not welcome at River Trace. Your brother was informed by our secretary that I would be making the call. He rang the office and left a message saying I shouldn't bother—he'd wait for you."

"That's ridiculous. And dangerous for the mare."

"I know. That's another reason I stopped by, to let you know." Haley gestured elegantly even with a callused hand. "It seems your brother doesn't like women."

"That's even more ridiculous." Lincoln was baffled. "He adores women. All sizes, all ages. And they love him."

"The wallflowers," Haley murmured. "But not my sort, the veterinarian sort. He made it clear he doesn't trust me to treat his horses. Nor will he give me the benefit of the doubt. In any case," she finished succinctly, "you might want to check on the mare."

"I will, thanks."

"Now I really have to run." Waggling her fingers, Haley said, "Cade, think of a perfect name." Addressing Linsey, she smiled. "You're fortunate. Judging by all I hear from Jesse, he's quite a boy. Like his dad, he'll be quite a man."

Another glance at the watch, and she exclaimed, "I'm late. Lincoln, Linsey, Cade—take care."

With that she left like a whirlwind, leaving a thunderous silence in her wake.

It was Linsey who finally spoke. "Is she always like that? So warm, so kind, so quick. So…?"

"So outspoken?" Lincoln added to the mix. "Always. She's also one of the most intelligent people I've ever known. Haley was one of the top students in our class." Lincoln gazed toward the door, where Haley had been. "Women who think chauvinism in medical schools is horrendous should try veterinary medicine."

"That's where you became friends, and why she's your partner?" Linsey had no trouble imagining how Lincoln would have befriended Haley Garrett. How he would've become her champion, making her life a little more tolerable. He'd done the same for her, and she'd fallen hopelessly in love with him. Had Haley? Was that why she'd come to Belle Terre?

"Haley's an army brat," Lincoln explained. "When her father was stationed at a base her parents didn't consider safe, she lived, briefly, in Belle Terre. With an elderly aunt, as I recall. From that time, she counted this part of the world, and Belle Terre, as the closest thing to a real home she'd ever had. The discovery and the coincidence of this common bond was the catalyst that drew us to each other at first."

That, Linsey thought, and Lincoln's innate gallantry toward any damsel in unhappy circumstances. As she was again. Wondering if there would ever be more between them, she smiled wryly. "Haley and I have both been fortunate in you."

"Lincoln," Cade called from his bed.

"Yeah, tiger." Drawn by the slight tremor in the boy's voice, he asked, "What do you need? Are you hurting?"

"No. I feel fine." The small, dark head ducked shyly.

"I've tried to be patient. Honest, I have." Gray eyes the exact duplicate of Lincoln's wandered to the book and the package. Fidgeting with the hem of his shirt, he blushed. "I was wondering..."

"If the book and the package were meant for you?" Moving to the bed, Lincoln cuffed an affectionate hand briefly around Cade's nape. "Of course they are. Who else would they be for?"

"I hoped for me. But since I messed up your boot, and your hat fell in the creek and I got blood all over your good shirt, I was afraid you'd think I didn't deserve anything."

"Messed up my boot? The trap did that, not you. The shirt's already washed clean as a whistle. And as far as the hat is concerned, it's salvageable." Realizing his mistaken choice of words, Lincoln corrected himself. "The hat can be fixed. I've taken it to be cleaned and blocked. It will be ready for you when you're ready for it."

Cade smiled then, and Linsey saw a healthy glow she knew had come to stay. "So I can open my presents?"

Lincoln gathered them from the table. As Cade took them, he looked first at the book on horses, his eyes wide. "They're so pretty. When I can read the words, will it tell me about them?"

"Sure will. When you're home, if you'd like, we can read it together," Lincoln offered.

Accepting that Lincoln would be in their home as if it were natural, Cade confessed, "You'll have to read, I'll look."

"That's a deal." Offering his hand, Lincoln waited until Cade gave him the high-five slap in his palm.

Cade was happily tearing the wrapping from the package, when Linsey admonished Lincoln. "You made it sound as if you'll be at the farm regularly."

"I will be, Linsey. You might as well understand now that I have every intention of being at the farm, as much as I can. Every morning, every night."

Linsey stared at him. Before she could speak, Cade was shrieking in delight. "A horse! Look, Mom! Lincoln gave me a statue of a horse. He's made of plastic so his legs move, but the saddle's leather. Next to Diablo and the colt, this must be the prettiest horse." A happy face turned to Lincoln. "It's the bestest gift I've ever got."

"I've got another surprise." Gathering up wrapping paper, Lincoln dropped it in the garbage. Setting the box aside, he waited for Cade's inevitable question. He wasn't disappointed.

"What kind of surprise, Lincoln?"

"How would you like for Jefferson to come visit? In fact, how would you like for him to spend the night tonight?"

"With my mom?" The boy was clearly puzzled.

"No, instead of your mom. She's been here constantly for five days. Now that you're so much better, I'd like to take her home for a quiet dinner and a good night's sleep in her own bed."

"Lincoln, no," Linsey protested, but neither Lincoln nor Cade noticed.

"Jefferson would really come?" Cade was intrigued.

"He said he would. In fact, he's eager to come. And I'll tell you a secret." Lincoln bent down to the boy, saying in a stage whisper, "Nobody tells better stories than Jefferson."

"About the swamp and the birds and animals he sees?"

"If that's what you want. But there's more. When Jefferson was sixteen or so, he spent two years working on a ranch in Arizona."

"He was a cowboy like Mr. Jesse?"

"Yep. That's where he met Jesse." Lincoln glanced at Linsey. He'd blindsided her, and she knew it. Without disappointing Cade, there was no way she could thwart Lincoln's plan. "The ranch was The Rafter B. The custom there was that when a cowboy broke his first horse, a special star was carved in his boot.''

''Did Jefferson get a star?''

''Sure did. Later he worked for a while for a saddle-bronc rider, too. The greatest in the world.''

''Do you think he'd tell me about that?''

Lincoln laughed. ''If the night's long enough. Does that mean you want him to come?''

''Sure.'' Sobering, Cade looked to his mother. ''If it's all right with Mom.''

Linsey wanted to say no. She wanted to refuse to go with Lincoln. But there were critical issues to be settled between them, and it was long past time. ''As long as it's truly all right with Jefferson.''

''It's a done deal as far as Jeffie's concerned.'' Lincoln checked the time. ''He should be here any minute.''

Heart racing and her breath stuttering in her lungs, Linsey turned to stare blindly at the river park below. The day she'd both feared and longed for had come at last.

# Eight

Heavy with promise for the end of a rainless period that threatened to become a summer drought, clouds building across the eastern sky roiled and seethed, reflecting the colors of sunset. A magnificent display Linsey didn't see.

She'd been quiet throughout the drive from the hospital. Quiet, still, her face composed. Except for the clench of her hands, this might be simply a tiresome trip she must endure.

"Relax," Lincoln said into a silence heightened by the steady hum of the engine of his truck. Then again, into the changing rumble of tires turning from the main road onto the narrow lane leading to the Stuart farm, he reminded her, "Jefferson's good with kids.

"Added to that, you've seen for yourself the staff at Belle Terre Trauma Center is top-notch in aftercare as well as treatment. Particularly Cooper's hand-picked team."

"Yes." The lifeless reply was lost in the groaning protests of the truck as it forded the stream meandering past

Stuart land. Tires spun, finding purchase as it lurched onto dry land.

No longer a neglected derelict, the Stuart house, the barn, and the small shed that housed Linsey's ancient car nestled in the clearing and shone in the slanting light. With a sense of belonging he hadn't known since Frannie Stuart's death, Lincoln let the truck roll to a halt before the front steps. The engine stopped, silence deepened within the cab, yet she gave no sign that she realized where they were. "We're home, Linsey."

She roused, her heart quickened at his choice of words. She didn't react. Her limbo was about to end. That much she knew, but not how. After weeks of agonizing over this encounter, she had discovered how and why no longer mattered. She was too exhausted to care about anything but her son.

"Cade will be all right."

"I know." And she did, yet her voice was unsteady.

"It's true." He took her hand in his. A small hand with a raw, newly healed scar across its palm. A hand bearing evidence of hardships she'd faced and met with strength and courage. Yet it lay lifeless in his. Touching her face, two fingers at her chin, he turned her to him. While she didn't resist, her lashes fluttered down like the rich gold fringe of a curtain, shielding her eyes from his probing inquisition.

"Open your eyes, Linsey." A tender command. "Open your eyes and look at me." A hush trembled between them. Deep and dark, magnified by the stillness of the farm and the whisper of a breeze stirring the tops of ancient trees. Lincoln waited.

Long seconds passed before her lashes lifted to lay bare her anguish. Lincoln knew he could lose himself in her eyes. His heart could rule his head if he moved too swiftly.

He'd seen trouble in those marvelous eyes for weeks. For weeks he'd fought the same battle. Time and again he'd wanted to forget the past, to pretend none of it happened. If there had only been the two of them to consider, perhaps he could have. But there was Cade. Wonderful, exuberant Cade. Whether they were to be friends, enemies or lovers, this day was about a child.

The child he'd known but a few weeks and yet, in that time, had become the reason for every choice he'd made. And, from this day, every choice he would make.

Meeting her worried gaze, watching the sun at his back spill light over her face, he wanted to take her in his arms to comfort her. But she was too distraught, too threatened, to be comforted by him.

Yet tonight he meant to bring their impasse to an end. Together they would find the right path to take for Cade.

*For my son.*

The words reverberated through his mind, an endless echo that threatened to spill from thought into words. Words he'd never dared say, even to himself, until this night.

Lincoln knew it was time. Stroking the jut of her chin, he smiled. "He will be, you know. Cade will be fine. Lucky laid the groundwork. Now it's up to us to do the rest. And we will, Linsey. We'll do it together."

Linsey moved in a dream. A dream, not a nightmare, because of Lincoln. Pausing in the doorway as he escorted her into her new home, she looked up at him. "You don't hate me." Wonder replaced worry in her eyes. "I think I would hate me."

"Why?" He needed to know, to understand.

"For what I denied you. For lost years. For my silence."

"I tried," Lincoln admitted. If this situation had any chance of resolution, they must both be honest. "That first night, when I struggled with the truth, I wanted to hate you. What I needed was to hate you and excuse myself. I couldn't absolve my fault in this then. I can't now."

"That first night." She moved into the front room that served as kitchen, dining, and family room in one. The heart of the Stuart home. "Cade saw a man on a horse. You and Diablo."

The kitchen was redolent with the scent of the meal Eden had had prepared at Lincoln's request. And, also at his request, Cullen had delivered. But Lincoln was hungry only for truths, for resolution. "In my mind I'd come to check for a pack of wild dogs. In my heart I was answering the call of nostalgia."

"Because of Lucky's letter." Hardly aware of her weariness, or of what she did, Linsey stretched out an unsteady hand to the arm of a chair for support and slipped into it.

"Because of both your letters." Lincoln was too restless to sit. Though he expended every effort not to prowl, he did, burning off the excesses of emotion as he paced the familiar room.

"How odd that they should arrive together. Lucky's trading on trust that your friendship had survived six years of silence. Eliciting a promise for me. Then mine saying Lucky had died. It must have been..." A shake of her head set her hair tumbling about her face as she stared down at the floor. "I can't even imagine how disturbing and puzzling it must have been.

"Yet he never mentioned Cade. Why?" she wondered, and Lincoln knew this bewildered and disturbed her.

"Not because he didn't love Cade. We both know that, Linsey." When she looked at him, her surprise evident, Lincoln explained, "I wouldn't have to see the two of them together to understand. All that's needed is to know Lucky as he was, and then Cade. Never doubt they loved each other. I never will."

"It's strange that he would ask favors on my behalf, knowing that if you complied, part of your responsibility would be Cade. A child he kept secret. He was lucid to the end, yet..." She shook her head again. "No matter how I try, it makes no sense."

"You're wrong." Lincoln stopped pacing, his gaze, pale as new silver, finding hers. "You're thinking in terms of Lucky alone. When I figure into the equation, it makes perfect sense."

He smiled then. A true smile, softening the line of his lips, warming his eyes. "When we were growing up, there were times Lucky knew me better than I knew myself. He knew how I would react, what I might say in unexpected circumstances.

"When my brothers and I were rebelling against Gus's iron hand, we worked from daylight till dark on the plantation, then ran wild all night. Burning the proverbial candle at both ends, raising hell, chasing the ladies. Lucky was never a part of it. But he didn't change. Through it all he was the same quiet, steady friend who knew me as well as my brothers. Sometimes better. Six years and three thousand miles didn't change that.

"Even facing death and in pain, he remembered I deal best with problems when I make my own decisions, in my own way, in my own time, with no preconceived opinions and ideas."

"Lucky didn't see Cade as a problem, Lincoln," Linsey objected. "On his worst days, Cade was the joy of his life."

"Of course he didn't," Lincoln agreed. "No one who knows Cade could ever doubt that. The problem, and the unknown, was me. How I would react. What I would do."

With another smile, one decidedly ironic, he continued, "Of course, that Lucky sent you here at all is a pretty clear indication he was dead certain how I would feel in the end."

"How is that?" Before her courage could fail, she asked again, "How *do* you feel about Cade?"

Lincoln turned away to stare out a window. The sun had dropped lower, sweeping shadows from the trees and rimming leaves with red-gold. Egrets, white feathers turned to creamy-rose in twilight, sailed low over the creek searching for one last meal before returning to roost. A whirling breeze driven before the seething heat of a wind storm plundered dry land and set dust devils dancing.

A tempest that would end, as had the tempest in Lincoln.

As he turned, his steady gaze found Linsey's. "I love him. I have from the first, even when I struggled with the truth. I spent the better part of a night downing a half bottle of scotch trying to deny that, in a single glimpse, a boy called Cade had turned my world upside down.

"The day I came to repair the steps, I knew what I felt had gone beyond denial. Though we'd only met, as we walked from the barn to the house, Cade took my hand. His trusting little fingers wrapping around mine wrapped tighter around my heart."

Lincoln looked away, a preoccupied expression on his face. He was a realist, quiet, pragmatic. A man who said little and chose his words carefully. Today he spoke from his captured heart. It was unsettling for one who guarded his emotions closely to speak so candidly of his feelings.

But he hadn't spoken out before, and he'd lost more than he ever dreamed possible. He wouldn't be reticent again.

Drawing himself from his contemplation, he faced Linsey again. The truth was there in his face for her to see as he spoke the words she'd never dared dream she would hear. "I love Cade, Linsey. I would've loved him no matter whose child he was. But I'm damned proud he's mine."

Linsey caught a breath, the first since he'd turned away. Relief flooded through her, tempered by the knowledge there was more to say. More to hear. More they both must face.

In a moment of quiet, a gaudy, ancient clock chimed a warning. As it ended, a silly little cuckoo Cade adored burst from its hiding place to chirp the hour. When it was done and shut securely behind tiny, carved doors until the next hour, the air seemed heavy and expectant.

Linsey roused as joy for Cade's gain became fear of her own loss. "What will you do, Lincoln? What do you want?"

"What do I want? To be a part of Cade's life—not just once in a while, but every day and every night. I want him to know me as the man I am. Not just the larger-than-life hero in Lucky's stories. Then, when the time is right, I want him to know himself—who he really is—and that I'm his father.

"When he knows and understands, the choice will be his."

"The choice!" Fear blazoned across Linsey's face in a disastrous assault, her fingers curled around the arms of her chair with a force that would have threatened less-sturdy construction. "You would take Cade from me?"

"Take Cade?" Lincoln was angered that she would consider him capable of such cruelty. "Of course I wouldn't. Dammit, I would never separate a child from the mother he adores."

Linsey had grown pale, her lips drawn taut and colorless. Her eyes, in contrast, seemed to burn with blue fire. Her exhaustion had become a living thing, consuming her. Yet Lincoln knew she would fight for Cade unto her last breath.

His anger abating, he left the window to come to her, taking the seat facing her. He'd been so caught up in his own reactions, he hadn't stopped to think that losing Cade would be her greatest fear. And yet, in the face of that fear, she had brought his son to him.

In the days of their friendship and as smoke-jumping partners, when the three of them knew each other better than anyone in the world, Linsey had always been strong. She'd always been kind. Above all, she'd been honest and honorable in all she did. Qualities he'd never doubted until she danced with a dark-haired child on the Stuart porch.

After that soul-shattering moment, even as he'd gone about his days keeping a promise he'd made in Lucky's memory, he wondered if he'd ever known her at all. Now she'd given him the most precious gift of all. At the risk of losing it herself.

There were questions to be asked and answers to be given by both of them. He would begin.

"I didn't mean to frighten you, sweetheart. It was stupid of me, but I didn't dream you would think I would do anything harmful to Cade. And that's what taking him from you would be. He's lost one person he loved, he shouldn't lose another.

"The choice I was speaking of, and the choice I would offer him, is his name. Stuart? Or Cade, his rightful surname."

Color returned to Linsey's face in slashes of rose across her cheeks. The glow should have become her, instead it emphasized the darkness that lay beneath her eyes like midnight shadows. "If he should choose Stuart?" Her fingers moved in a nervous rhythm. "If he prefers to remain Cade Stuart, what then?"

"If that's the choice he makes, I'll abide by it. Thanks to you and to Lucky, Cade's a son any father would be proud of. I can only hope and pray he chooses to be known as mine."

Linsey knew the choice her son would make. The same choice Lucky had intended from the beginning he would make if given the opportunity. Lucky's way of coping with his conscience was to teach Cade to love his true father before he ever knew him.

Then Lincoln, the man he was, and had always been, fulfilled every promise Lucky's stories made.

Yet there was more to this for all of them than just a name. Perhaps life should be that simple, but Linsey knew from her own experiences it never was. "How will you explain to those who matter that suddenly you have a son?"

The steady gray gaze that had always seemed to see into her soul, save once, captured hers. "With the truth," he said calmly and matter-of-factly. "When I know it."

"Yes." Linsey agreed, the truth was the place to begin a life that, from this day forward, would never be the same. "Shall I begin now?"

"You're exhausted, Linsey. I brought you home to rest and to eat something beside hospital fare. We've said enough. The rest can be left for another day. Instead, we should sample the delicacies Eden's chef prepared for us."

"I can't." As the burden of years of guilt lifted a bit, if not completely, the last of the strength she'd begged, borrowed and stolen from every reserve deserted her. With it her appetite, as was common. She'd never been so spent.

She'd struggled and persisted as long as there were lonely battles to be fought. Now there was Lincoln. Cade had a strong, healthy father to guide him, to protect him. In relinquishing a part of that responsibility, she'd let down her guard, and bone-deep weariness she'd denied for years struck like an impatient assassin.

A glance at the kitchen and the table set so prettily with Frannie Stuart's keepsakes and finished with a small basket of gifts, topped with a single summer lily, drew a sad frown from her. Eden and Cullen had done this, at Lincoln's request, for her. Rare kindnesses she hadn't the strength to accept.

"I'm sorry." Tears gathered in her eyes and trembled on the tips of her lashes. She hated the weakness, hated that she couldn't cope. "For this. For being so weak. For everything."

Lincoln realized she was at the end of her endurance. But in it he didn't see weakness. Instead he saw great strength. The sort of warriors who fought too long and too hard, until it was the body that crumbled beneath a spirit that would fight on.

"I'm the one who should be sorry. I bring you home for

desperately needed rest, then subject you to this.'' Rising from his chair and taking her hand, he drew her up with him. ''Food can wait for another day, too. What you need is a glass of Eden's best wine and a long soak in the tub.''

Linsey didn't argue. It sounded like heaven.

''There's a storm coming. Mostly hot winds have been predicted. Some thunder and lightning. Maybe, but strongly doubtful, for the lucky ones, the rain the whole countryside needs. While you soak, I'll put away the food and clear the table. After that I should ride over to Belle Reve to see if Jesse needs help with the horses. The only thing that spooks Jackson's Arabians worse than thunder and lightning is wind. The old cowhand would never admit it, but he might need help tonight.''

''Will you go to River Trace?'' Though she'd never seen it, in the hours she'd spent watching over her son, she'd learned quite a lot about Jackson Cade's River Trace. From Cade's chatter she knew the handsome bachelor lived in only a part of the old plantation manor, while he waited for the remainder of the house to be restored. It was at River Trace he stabled his Irish stock.

''Only long enough to check the mare. I spoke with Jackson earlier. Since Jefferson's at the hospital with Cade, Merrie Alexandre volunteered to help his men with the stock. Unless the mare's in labor, with the girl around he won't need anyone else. It's true that only Jesse and Jefferson, and maybe Jackson, can handle horses better than Eden's little gaucho.''

From the look on Linsey's face, Lincoln knew he should explain. ''Merrie's the daughter of a friend of a friend of Eden's. She's staying and working at the Inn while she attends the local college. Her father's a fantastically wealthy businessman in Argentina who believes strongly in two things—that everyone should learn the value of working, including his only daughter, and that a lady should be a lady first, a horsewoman second, and never, ever, one of the guys or gauchos. Especially his daughter.''

"So he sends her here, and she ends up helping out at a horse ranch." Linsey smiled at the irony.

"Only with her father's permission and Eden's guidance.''

"If anyone can make a lady of Mr. Alexandre's daughter, I would say it's Eden Cade,'' Linsey ventured.

Lincoln would have added another name to that list, but Linsey needed a hot soak and the wine more than she needed compliments she wouldn't accept. Gently he urged her toward that bath. "Take Eden's basket. Try the bath oil. It's Cullen's creation. His adaptation of *Umu Hei Monoi,* an oil commonly used on his native island. As Eden understands the qualities of a lady, our own Pacific Islander understands the magic of fragrance.''

"Cullen's creation?'' In her wandering days, Linsey had spent a summer in the Pacific and had recognized his accent. But it was difficult to imagine the great Goliath delving into the art of blending delicate scents.

"Yes, Cullen's. That's only one of his many astonishing skills.'' Lincoln didn't explain that in Cullen's island tales, *Umu Hei Monoi* was the perfume of Aphrodite.

A sudden gust of wind rattled windows and knocked at the door as if to announce that more would come calling soon. "If you go along now, you have time for a good soak. But should there be unexpected thunder, lightning won't be faraway. At the first crack, get out of the tub immediately. By then you should be ready for a restful sleep. I'll be back pretty late…''

"You're coming back?'' Linsey interrupted.

"I said I'd be here every day and every night, Linsey. And I meant it,'' Lincoln explained patiently. "Starting tonight.''

"There're only two bedrooms.''

"No one knows that better than I. That's why I plan to

bed down in the tack room in the barn.'' He spoke of the room once used for farm equipment, converted now into temporary lodgings for whichever of Jackson's men drew night duty when horses were finally stabled in the Stuart barn. ''I would sleep there if there were three bedrooms in the house. I don't want to wake you when I'm called away in the night.

''Now.'' He drew her to him, kissed her forehead, then released her. ''About that bath.''

Fragrant steam rose from froth that lay over the surface of the water. Bubbles, capturing the reflected flame of the single candle Linsey had chosen in lieu of the bright glare of the utilitarian ceiling bulb, danced over her skin, anointing her in scented light. Heat seeped into deep, tightly coiled muscles, releasing tensions in mind as well as body. Leaning back, eyes closed, she gave herself up to the magic Lincoln promised.

She had no concept of time, no idea how long she'd drifted in this sweet nirvana, when a soft tap sounded at the door.

Had Lincoln returned? Had he not gone? Unable to muster an answer in her sweet lassitude, she murmured. ''Yes?''

''Are you decent?''

Looking down at herself, swathed in scintillating bubbles from her chin to her toes, she chuckled. A sound absent too long in her life and the life of the man who waited beyond the door. ''If you call bubbles that multiply by the minute and smell like heaven, of course I'm decent.''

The laughter was still in her voice and in her eyes when Lincoln stepped inside. Catching back a gasp, he realized that, even in the early days, even before Cade, he'd never seen her so relaxed. Nor so beautiful.

Her hair had been drawn into a coil at the crown of her head, and surely had begun to tumble free immediately.

Tousled and shining tendrils curled around her face and drifted to her shoulders. Heat brought color back to her lips and face, lending a healthy glow. The golden rosiness of her cheeks turned her eyes the splendid sapphire he'd seen only in that rare, fleeting moment at sunset at the end of stormy days.

She was so desirable it was agony not to reach out and take her. God help him, it would be so easy to throw caution to the wind. To forget everything—the past, the future. Everything but Linsey wrapped in the seductive scent of *Umu Hei Monoi.*

Reining in lust and need that lay hot and unquenchable in him, he stepped closer. Trying not to see that the slope of her breasts, just visible above the white froth, were creamy and fuller than he remembered. Or that beads of oil gathered like exotic jewels in the cleft of their fullness, enticing him to wonder what it would be like to lave away each tiny sphere and discover the blend of their taste with her skin.

Perhaps it was true that beauty lay in the eyes of the beholder. True or not, in his eyes Linsey Blair had always been lovely. But never as lovely as in the bloom of maturity.

*Blair.* Lincoln realized his error. In the throes of the spell she cast, he'd stepped back in time. But she was no longer Linsey Blair. She hadn't been for six years.

With that realization came the resurrection of sanity.

"I didn't mean to intrude, but Eden made it a special point to ask that you try a glass of her favorite wine. She laughed when she said it, then added quite seriously that a soak in Cullen's magic potion and a flute of this particular vintage could work miracles." Setting the bottle on a table within her reach, he waited until she took the fragile flute. Her fingers brushed his as they curled lazily around the delicate stem. Only a touch and all he'd fought to deny was alive and urgent again.

Her eyes were heavy lidded and as dreamy as her voice when she asked, "Why are you doing this, Lincoln? Why would you be so kind after what I've done?"

For the space of a calming breath, Lincoln couldn't answer, then the truth came pouring out. "Perhaps because I think there's more to this than meets the eye. Extenuating circumstances beyond all our control. Perhaps because if there's guilt in this, a greater portion is mine."

"You can't know, Lincoln." A sense of urgency overcame the lassitude that enveloped her. "You don't understand. I haven't lied to you, but you don't know the truth."

"You're wrong, Linsey. I do understand. And the only truth that matters is that you're the mother of my child."

"Lincoln."

"Shhh." He sealed her lips with his fingers. "Enjoy your bath. I'll be back late, but I'll see you in the morning. Cooper's releasing Cade. We'll bring him home, together."

"Cade's coming home?"

Lincoln crossed the room and, pausing in the doorway, he smiled. "Tomorrow."

Linsey didn't know how long she listened to the whisper of the wind as enchanting oils worked their magic. An hour? Two? However long, the water had grown cool, the bubbles had dissipated, when she stepped from the tub.

Laughing softly, she swayed giddily, reaching for a towel. A glance proved the decanter was empty. Dismay was short-lived as she laughed again. "Lincoln's fault. He did this. All his fault."

After a halfhearted swipe at the sheen of moisture clinging to her, she dropped the towel and walked down the hall to her bedroom. Twilight was slipping into the first gentle graying of night, but a lamp by her bed lit her way. The dry, hot wind that had buffeted the old house in sporadic gusts still moaned and sighed and rustled in the trees. As she drew on a demure gown of cotton lawn, washed thin and faded to palest blue, she stopped to listen, wondering what secrets the wind whispered.

Letting the long gown fall to the tops of her bare feet, not caring that droplets of fragrant bath water caught at the fabric, she crossed to the window. A light shone beyond the shutters of the tack room. Lincoln had returned.

Trailing her fingertips over heated panes, feeling the thrum of another rush in their sensitized tips, she wondered if winds like this had come knocking at the same windows, whispering secrets to Lincoln when he was a boy like Cade.

"Secrets," she murmured. "Secrets that mustn't be secrets any longer."

Suddenly she was running, unmindful of fragrant oil still clinging to her. Not caring that those sweet droplets caught at the thin, faded fabric of her gown, turning it to gossamer, she ran to Lincoln.

# Nine

The wind was a steady force laced with stronger gusts, thrusting Linsey forward as if urging her on. As she passed it by, an old garden gate bumped in an uneven rhythm, straining against new hinges. Beyond the garden that waited for caring hands and rain, the old barn, resplendent in new paint, groaned and creaked like an ancient, arthritic creature.

The unfettered fire of the low-riding moon marked her way over dry grass and past reconstructed corrals. Spilling through the open barn door, it lay like a silver trail ending in cloistering shadows. Linsey ran on as dust sifted from the loft, and the scent of Jackson's new-mown hay became the perfume of the sultry, summer night. As she passed empty stalls ready for Arabians, only a sliver of light seeping beneath the tack room door served as her guide.

A heated blast buffeted the barn again. Somewhere in the night an owl called to another as something furry skittered over Linsey's bare foot. Her stifled scream was nearly lost in the wail of the wind, but it was enough that Lincoln heard.

The door was flung open, light enveloped her like a beacon. Still frightened and unsettled, her eyes shining darkly with the remnants of alarm, she didn't know that her hair cascaded about her in mad disarray. Caught in a storm of conflicting emotions, she didn't care that a mist of fragrant oil still clung to her, catching back the threadbare fabric the instant she stepped beyond the lash of the wind.

As she stared mutely at Lincoln, in the stifling heat of the barn, simple cotton had become translucent, cleaving to her.

"Linsey?" Lincoln stood in the doorway, dressed only in jeans riding low over his hips, with a towel draped around his neck. The last thing he'd expected was visitors. Especially Linsey in the guise of this fey, maddening blue-eyed gypsy.

He waited for her response. Disturbed, entranced, aware of little but Linsey, beyond the rise and fall of his breathing he hardly moved. A sheen of moisture reflected the flickering glow of a lantern. Rimmed in mellow luminescence, half in light, half in shadow, his body became burnished umber, his hair gleaming ebony.

In the days he'd worked on the farm, keeping that careful distance, Linsey had never seen him in any state of undress. In the hottest of lowcountry temperatures, Lincoln was well groomed, his attire proper for each day's particular chore. A rugged, unstudied decorum that made him even more inaccessible. In the roughest of clothing, he'd worn the aura of careless charm ever the lot of true Southern gentlemen. But neither charm nor the male beauty he would despise and deny could have prepared her for the virile splendor of Lincoln Cade half-naked.

As he slid the towel from his neck, she watched lamplight play over the muscles of his chest and arms. Muscles that rippled beneath taut, sun-darkened skin with the grace of vigor and guarded power. Then he was more than beautiful, more than splendid. With his shirt cast aside and his close-cropped hair tousled, he was gloriously uncivilized, utterly magnificent.

Reading his concern, Linsey couldn't respond. Her eyes held his as she stood without the power to reassure him.

"Linsey?" Alarm rasped in his tone. "What's wrong?" New tension scored his features like a frown. "Dear God! Is it Cade?"

Shaking her head, setting windblown hair ashimmer, she tried to speak. She wanted to explain, but could only make the same mute denial.

"Are you hurt…?" Lincoln took a panicked step toward her. But, afraid that if she were hurt he might hurt her more, he didn't touch her. "Please, Linsey. Tell me."

"Lincoln."

There was anguish in her voice and in his name. But like her scream, it was enough as he recognized the regret in her eyes, the heartache. He didn't question again as he reached for her, drawing her into his arms. As her body molded the muscular planes of his, he tamed the wild disorder of her hair. Letting his lips trail over her temple, scarcely aware of what he said, he soothed her with soft words and sweet endearments. "Easy, my love, don't think about anything. Don't worry about anything. I'm here, sweetheart. I'll always be here, and there's nothing to fear."

"Lincoln, I have to tell you." She lifted her face from his shoulder, her expression tense. "You have to know about Cade."

"I know, Linsey." Gathering her back to him, his fingers tangled again in her bewitching, golden hair as if he would keep her forever. "I think I've known from the first. For too long I was too stubborn and too damnably proud to admit I was as much to blame in this as you or Lucky." He caught back a ragged sigh. "That isn't true. The greatest fault in all of this is mine. Because of it, I deserved the price I paid."

"No!" Linsey would have said more, but the brush of his lips against hers swept every protest and denial from her mind.

Straightening, moving only a half step away, from his greater height Lincoln looked down at her. Remembering the hurt, brave young girl she'd been in times of danger. Seeing the braver woman she'd become as she'd coped with a greater hurt and then the duress of Lucky's illness, his heart filled with pride. Pride in the mother of his son, the woman he'd abandoned like a callow fool. The woman he'd never ceased to desire beyond all reason.

"The past doesn't matter." His voice was low and unsteady, steeped in desire and passion. "Nothing matters now but Cade." Almost too softly to be heard he added, "And you."

This time, though he no longer touched her, when he bent to kiss her, his lips lingered. As he teased with unhurried fervor, one kiss led to two. Two kisses to another. Until he drew her back to him. "This little time is ours. I can't sully it with remembering the grief and guilt of yesterday, or by anticipating the worries of tomorrow. It doesn't matter what went before. We're older and wiser. We can deal with whatever may come.

"But for now there's only this minute," he muttered into her hair. "And, God help me, as before, there's only this."

Linsey didn't object when he swept her off her feet to take her to his lodgings for the night. Nor when he kicked the door closed, sealing them in the small, rough space. If God must help Lincoln, He must help her, too, for she wouldn't object, no matter what he said or didn't say. No matter what he did.

She wanted the passion, the unbridled sex, the lust. She wanted the urgency she felt in his kiss and in his touch. She needed as much as wanted the exorcism of guilt and grief in mindless passion. As she needed to revel in Lincoln's desire, no matter that it was lust, never love. Now or in the past.

When he set her on her feet, his hands slipping from her
waist to her hips as he took a final step fitting his hard body
to hers, she knew everything he said was true. Beyond
Cade, nothing mattered but Lincoln. As her palms touched
his bare chest she was vaguely aware that no scent of horses
clung to him. She knew then he'd bathed in the creek before settling down for the night. Had he thought of her bath
and the seductive fragrance of Cullen's magic oil as he
bathed? Had he known then she would come to him?
Would he have come to her if she hadn't?

Then his mouth was seeking hers, less tenderly now in
the hunger of desperation. Greedily her lips parted, opening
to the intimate caress of his, and the essence of Lincoln
filled her world. His scent. His taste. His touch. Lincoln
with his hair tousled and damp and gleaming beneath her
roving fingers. Lincoln, magnificent with his body still wet
from the stream.

"Lincoln," she whispered again as he lifted his lips from
hers. *Lincoln, my love. My only love,* her thoughts echoed
in her heart as she held him. In the hush of passion the
only sound was the keening of the wind, then she didn't
think at all.

It was Lincoln who drew away because he needed to
look at her, to cherish the longing in her eyes a little longer.
Then, tearing his gaze from hers, he sought the secrets of
her body. Secrets he'd known only once, yet remembered
as vividly as if only a day had passed. In lamplight her
gown was breathtaking because it was she who wore it.
Sensible cotton that should have been demure enticed because it was to her body it clung, offering glimpses of paradise.

But his need was beyond this sweet pleasure, his thirst
for her demanded more. A hand that was far less steady
than one would expect of calm, pragmatic Lincoln Cade
traced the line of her throat, then the slope of her breast.
As he stroked the shadowed cleft, he felt her shudder spiral
through him, as well.

Beyond the shelter of the barn, the wind began to weaken. Sealed away from the weather and the world, the small, primitive room grew stiller, hotter, more sultry. In the rising temperature the islander's mystical potion wrapped him in its fragrance. It was then Lincoln believed that, blended with Linsey's own natural scent, it was truly the perfume of Aphrodite.

Cupping her breasts with his palms, his gliding fingertips went where his lips hungered to be. Her breasts were full for her small size but perfect for his hands. Dragging his gaze from the fascinating changes his touch could bring to her body, he discovered Linsey trembled as she watched him through eyes darkened by unfathomable desire. ''I want to see you, Linsey. All of you. I want to touch you, not cloth, no matter how it becomes you.'' His voice had grown deeper in the heat of desire. ''I need you. This time I won't hurt you. I'll never hurt you again.''

Linsey couldn't move. Nor could she deny him, if denial had been her wish. Lincoln had said the perfect words. All but the single word she wanted to hear. Her darkened gaze searched his beloved face as she relived the past. *Bittersweet.* With Lincoln she'd taken the bitter with the sweet. If that was all there was to be, she would again. Eyes downcast, hiding her sorrow, she raised unsteady fingers to the tiny buttons at her throat.

''No.'' Lincoln brushed her hands away. ''Let me.'' There were tears in her eyes as he slipped the first button from its delicate loop. One after the other each button slipped free. Then the task was done, and the gown drifted to the bare floor. For a long while he could only stare at her. ''Do you know, Linsey?'' His gaze moved from her body to her mouth, then her eyes. ''I wonder, could you ever know how lovely you are?''

''I'm not beautiful or lovely or any such thing.'' The ugly duckling no one wanted had not, would not, miraculously turn into a swan. ''I can only be what I am, and I will never be beautiful, Lincoln. Not even for you.''

"Ah, but you are." He cradled her head, his thumbs stroking her cheeks, then the corners of her mouth. "It's going to be my life's work to make you believe." Bending to her, he touched her lips with his. His hands slipped down her bare back. Then he had her in his arms, taking her to the single bunk to lay her on a mattress of new straw covered in rough ticking. In dancing lamplight he stood feasting on beauty she couldn't believe. But she would. He would teach her. Reaching for the snap of his jeans, he murmured softly. "Starting now, love. Now."

*Love.* He gave her the name as if it were true. Yet never spoke the words she'd given her soul to hear once before, and would again. But never to any avail. Low and hoarsely she whispered the truth as she knew it and would accept it. "Never."

"Yes." Lincoln misinterpreted the single word as he came down to the bunk to begin her seduction.

His kiss was a fierce claim, his mouth hot and clever, seeking responses she couldn't deny. Linsey writhed as each touch and each kiss branded her, making her his, if only in lust. Desire had burned within her like a steady flame. Now it was wildfire consuming her, driving her mad. With a sigh she moved against him, seeking, needing. Grasping his hair, not caring that her clasp might be painful, she dragged his mouth to her own. Then caution was lost. She touched as he touched, claimed as he claimed. Until Lincoln caught her hands, keeping them. "Witch." He growled softly. "Drive me crazy, would you?"

"Yes," she muttered and in her mind added, *crazy with love for me, if only I could.*

"Then, my sweet. Two can play that game." Reining in desire that had moved too far, too quickly, Lincoln began again the slow, delightful seduction he'd intended. With wandering touches he teased her throat, the tilt of her breasts, and their budding crests. With kisses he soothed the torment, only to create more. As her body arched, lifting her breasts to his caress, instead he buried his face in their cleft. Breathing in the scent of Linsey anointed with *Umu Hei Monoi* he was seduced himself.

Turning his head, catching a nipple between his lips, he drew the tiny tip deeper into his mouth. The rasp of his tongue provoked, aroused. Linsey trembled in response and called his name. In the sound there was sweet dementia. It was the note Lincoln had waited to hear. The moment for which all that had gone before had been intended.

A cry that beguiled him, and he acknowledged it by sinking into her embrace. Bodies joining in the first exquisite pleasure, they moved together. On a crude wooden bunk history replayed itself as, in the soaring threat of a storm, in stifling heat, their skin grew slick, emotions more liberated, responses frenzied. Tension mounted, moving to another plane. Until Linsey went still and breathless in concert with the hushed cry torn from Lincoln. And passion shattered into nirvana.

Though it had gone unnoticed, all the while the wind had been calming. Now as if it would make one last statement, its dying rush battered the sturdy old walls and snaked through the center passage. Half doors of stalls lining each side rattled and strained. But, reinforced and repaired, and with new latches in preparation for livestock, each only shook and clattered, then calmed one by one as the mischievous breeze passed them by.

The last, the door to the tack room, never meant to withstand the pummeling of a thousand-pound horse, or an intruding wind, was easier prey. Hinges held, but the worn latch slipped free. The door imploded, banging and rebounding back and forth before settling against the wall.

As if chuckling at the success of its last hurrah, the breeze snaked on. By the time it reached the corral, it had only the strength to rattle a rusty chain left hanging on a fence post. Then the trees were still. The clearing, but for bright leaves and small limbs torn free and strewn across it, was as it had been.

The barn was silent. Unaware of this final foray, sated

and exhausted, two lovers held each other as if even in sleep they dared not let go.

When Lincoln woke he lay on the narrow bunk alone.

"Linsey?" As she turned from the open door, he saw with regret that she'd drawn the faded gown over the body he'd loved, then loved again through the night. "What are you doing?"

"It's raining. Or it will be soon. Now there's only the mist," she said as if that would explain everything, while she resumed her watch of the early-morning haze.

Swinging his long legs over the edge of the bunk, Lincoln reached for his jeans. That she'd dressed seemed to demand that he should, too. Padding barefoot to her to stand at her back with his arms circling her waist, he caught her against him.

Leaning into his embrace, Linsey's hands folded over Lincoln's as his fingers splayed over the flat plane of her stomach. The first time they'd made love, by morning Cade was a tiny, infinitesimal being. But she'd had no inkling of him then, or even for months later. God help her, indeed, if history truly repeated itself.

Lincoln had used no protection. He was obviously not a man who went ever prepared. She'd tried the pill and other treatment for the irregular menses diagnosed first by one physician as being caused by the stringent smoke-jumpers' training. Then by another as the exorbitant stress and danger of parachuting into infernos. Nothing worked. There was no cure. Her menses remained erratic. Sometimes coming too frequently for too long, then not at all for months.

When Lucky's health deteriorated so rapidly birth control wasn't necessary, she'd stopped all treatment. What need had she for birth control now, when she never expected to have another man in her life? Never, in her wildest dreams, would she have foreseen the need to prepare for an interlude like last night.

An interlude with lasting consequences? she wondered.

Then, to her surprise and shame, and in spite of the past, she found herself hoping it could be true.

No! Sanity reasserted itself. Another child conceived out of mistaken passion rather than love would only be a tragic complication in a situation already far too complicated. Linsey looked down at their hands lying over her stomach. Hers chafed and reddened from unaccustomed labor around the farm. Lincoln's darker, rougher from year after year of harder, far more grueling work. Yet wonderfully beautiful, holding her out of caring and rekindled desire. But never in love.

Heart aching, Linsey abandoned foolish dreams. Another child could not, must not be, no matter how she might wish it.

With a turn of her head, her hair tumbled over one shoulder and lay against her breast. Never one to miss an inadvertent invitation, bending to drop a line of kisses from her shoulder to her exposed nape, Lincoln muttered, ''Pretty,'' as his tongue stroked the spot he'd discovered would make her shiver. He wasn't disappointed. Hoarsely, already aroused and aching for her so soon, he whispered again, ''So pretty.''

Forcing herself from the abyss of regret, hardly aware that Lincoln kissed her, or even that she'd shivered as he'd wished, she looked again to the new day. ''Is there anything prettier than a misty morning?''

A gruff denial rumbled in his chest. Lincoln turned her in his arms, his hand at her chin raised her gaze to his. ''I meant you, Linsey. You're the pretty one. Pretty here and here.'' With each word Lincoln traced the shape of her face.

''Most of all, here.'' His fingers slipped down her throat to rest over her heart. ''You're too pretty here to blame all the bastards who've hurt you. You look for reasons within yourself—that you weren't pretty enough or smart enough or kind enough—excusing the parents who abandoned you, the foster homes that did little better. And even me.''

When she would speak, he framed her face between his

palms, "Don't," he insisted. "Don't make excuses for any of us. Don't look for some fault in yourself that will absolve me.

"Name me the irresponsible bastard I deserve to be called, and I'll agree with you. But say you aren't blameless, that you aren't beautiful, and I'll argue until my dying breath."

Linsey said nothing. She'd never seen him so angry, so determined. She had no intention of calling Lincoln any names, nor would she interrupt this diatribe on her world and himself.

"What the people responsible for your childhood did was bad enough. What I did—" Breaking off, in his agitation a hand raked roughly through his hair. For a long while he gazed down at her, as rain pattered hollowly on the roof. "What I did was unconscionable. I took your innocence, then walked away."

"You were injured, Lincoln. You didn't know…"

"In the final diagnosis it was only a mild concussion, Linsey," he cut her off. "No matter how demented I might have seemed at other times, I knew exactly what I was doing when I made love to you. I knew it was wrong. The wrong time, the wrong place, the wrong reason. To my everlasting shame that didn't stop me. I'm not sure anything could have.

"Later, when Lucky looked me in the eyes, I felt as if he could see the black of my soul. He knew I'd done a terrible thing, yet he didn't speak of it. Instead, he admitted he loved you, that he had for a long time. And, like a coward, I backed away."

"You make it sound as if you forced me to make love with you." Shock darkened Linsey's gaze, but with it came a glimmer of understanding. "It was never like that, Lincoln. Never."

"No?" He wouldn't be dissuaded. "I wanted you. I needed you so badly. I didn't think of anything else. Not even the hurt I might cause you."

Pausing, he remembered the fire and the fear. Fear, not of dying, but of never having truly lived. Of never having loved Linsey. Of never teaching her the ways of love and loving. "The fire unleashed the need I'd fought so long to keep hidden, and I was afraid." The admission was made with abject honesty, as only a strong man would dare. "I was afraid it would be my last and only chance. All I could think was that *I* wanted. *I* needed. And as selfishly as that, knowing beyond a doubt that your compassionate heart would not refuse my needs, damn my soul, I took."

"You took nothing that wasn't yours for the taking. Nothing I didn't give willingly and need as badly." Nothing a single no wouldn't have protected and preserved. But she hadn't said no then. She hadn't now, when he needed her once again.

Linsey wanted to hold him, to make him believe that if there was fault, it was fault they shared. But his story was not done. She knew, without understanding how she knew, that until it was told in its entirety his self-condemnation would not end. So she listened, and loved him, but did not touch him.

"When I stepped aside for Lucky, in my mind I was stepping aside for a better man. And trying to escape the guilt I could barely face. Hell, I was so sure I knew what was best for all of us. Yet I hated the idea of Lucky having you so badly that before the wedding I ran away." All for want of the words he craved but was afraid to speak himself.

"You didn't know I was pregnant with your child."

"I didn't stick around long enough to find out, did I? Ever?" With an emphatic turn of his head he answered his own question. "No. It was all about me. *My* guilt. *My* shame. With never a concern for what the consequences of making love might be for you, I took off, even dropping out of jumpers season early.

"Then I waltzed back into your life two months later to

serve in a father's stead. Hurting even as I gave you to Lucky. And still I didn't ask the questions I should have.''

"I couldn't have answered, Lincoln. Not when I had no reason to suspect any change. Lucky and I had been married a month when I knew I was carrying your child. There were no signs, no problems. Not even..." Linsey searched for a simple way to explain erratic workings of intimate body functions.

"I know," Lincoln said, sparing her, reading the bewilderment on her face. "That shouldn't surprise you. Think about it. How could I not know when we lived in such close contact? Always the three of us, working, eating, sleeping together, sometimes for weeks without a break. Bathing when we could, where we could. Attending to physical needs—if they occurred.

"Of course I knew. So did Lucky. Hell, Linsey, after weeks of training each year and three summers of working together as a team, even the most obtuse idiot in the world would have known.''

Her eyes widened as slashes of color crept in her cheeks and her throat in stunned embarrassment.

"That shocks you?" A half smile barely moved his lips. A knuckle ruffled the coarse, old-fashioned lace at the edge of a tuck in the bodice of her gown. "As modest as you are, I expect it does." After a considering pause, he added regretfully, "Then let me add another shocker to the cause. Lucky knew about us. The more I think about it, factoring in the awful knowledge of his illness, he sensed the change in us.

"He was the true hero, we both know that, Linsey. But survivors share a unique bond. We had always been the Three L's, each an equal part of the relationship.''

Beginning to understand, Linsey took up the story. "Then we spent three days in an isolated shack, never knowing if we would be alive or dead from one hour to the next.''

Cupping her cheek, remembering her courage, his thumb

skimmed over the skin beneath her eyes as if he would erase the mark of fatigue. "Three days when you suffered the worst of the worry while I was less than lucid much of the time. We lived because of Lucky. He was the hero. But we had more—more even than the bond of survivors, for even as we faced death, we shared the gift of living as lovers."

"At the worst time in his life, he felt shut out." Pain shone in Linsey's eyes. "I can imagine how much it hurt."

"That he didn't explain to us that his protracted stay in the hospital was for more than burns and smoke inhalation, tells a part of it. I can understand his despair when, in the first selfish act of his life, he reached for the brass ring. For you, Linsey."

"He couldn't know what you would do." Linsey still found it difficult to believe Lucky could scheme so deliberately.

"He did. I'd backed away before, when I knew there was something he wanted. Because I felt I owed it to him. The difference this time was a greater debt. He'd just been given a death sentence of the worst kind for a man like Lucky—long, slow, without dignity. I think any man might go crazy with that. Yes, he knew I would step aside and, damn me, I did.

"And the destruction of any future we might have salvaged was complete. I left you to believe that what I'd done was only lust. I was the history of your young life repeating itself. One more person who turned away from you." He drew a ragged breath as he spoke the old, hurtful lie. "One more person who didn't want you."

"But Lucky did," she finished for him, believing now. "That's why he was depressed, rather than angry, when I realized I was pregnant. Why he insisted the child be called Cade. Why he taught Cade to love you from the beginning. And why, at the last, he made me promise I would bring Cade here."

"He was making amends by giving my son to me." This time it was Lincoln who finished for Linsey.

"He couldn't be sure I would keep my word. That I would come." Linsey looked away from Lincoln. The sun was fully risen, and rain had begun to fall in earnest. Rain and sunshine, a contradiction, like Lucky Stuart.

"He couldn't know I would risk…" In distress, she'd nearly said risk her heart to Lincoln again. As she searched for another explanation, Lincoln spoke.

"He knew." Turning her gaze from the rain, Lincoln smiled. "He knew everything. How each of us would react, then and now. His trump card was that he knew your history. That you were a foundling, raised in foster homes, an orphanage, then strict catholic schools. He knew Linsey Blair was the woman you created, with a name you chose, taken from your favorite nun and the phonebook. You had no roots, no family; no one in all your life ever made you feel wanted."

"Except Lucky." And once, for a while, Lincoln. Now he wanted her again, for Cade.

"He was a good friend and an unselfish man whose life had suddenly gone haywire. He was still grieving for Frannie, and a long way from recovery. Then came the fire and the burns and learning his life, as he knew it, was over. We were the last straw."

"How did he recognize what was between us? What difference did he see?"

"He loved you, Linsey. He saw everything about you. Every nuance and every change." Softly he added, "If it had been you and Lucky in that shack in Oregon, I would have known."

But Lucky had only taken what Lincoln hadn't wanted. When he discovered there was more, more than being second choice… "He made it right," she said in a whisper as Lincoln brushed away a fallen tear. "Shortly before the wedding, he told me of his illness and offered to set me free.

"He always made it right. That's why Lucky's short life focused on giving your son and your son's love back to you."

"Not just my son, Linsey. Our son. Whether we're together or apart, that's how it's going to be."

"For Cade."

"Who's coming home today." He saw sadness mixed with joy and offered a diversion. "We need to find Brownie."

"You brought him back from Belle Reve." She'd heard the dog bark in the night, then had forgotten. "Where is he now?"

"Out reacquainting himself with the farm and looking for Cade. We'll call him in and dry him off later."

"Dry him off? Why?"

"He's going with us to get Cade. That should make them both happy. Don't you think?"

"I think, yes." A small gesture, but one that touched Linsey and made her heart soar. Lincoln would be a wonderful father. Lucky had been right in sending the boy home to him.

"Hey, don't look so serious. Beginning with today we're starting over. We'll work it out. Whatever's best for Cade we'll do. In the meantime, have you ever danced in the rain?"

Linsey looked up at Lincoln as if he'd lost his mind.

"No?" Clasping her hand in his, he grinned. The teasing, wicked grin she'd fallen in love with years before.

"Never," she answered wistfully.

"Then, my love," he laughed as he tugged her toward the clearing. "It's past time you did."

# Ten

Cade laughed and Brownie barked deliriously. A boy and his dog, exploring the world, happy with life and each other. Trowel in hand, Linsey stopped digging in the black soil of the flower garden. Tipping back on her heels, she crouched there listening.

Once she'd feared it would be a long while before she would hear that familiar sound again. But she'd underestimated her son's determination and the power of Lincoln's influence. She understood now how hero worship worked. Each day she realized a little more that Cade felt he had to be like the man who had become the focus of his life. So he had done what he thought Lincoln would do with a broken leg, accepting his lot with a "grin and bear it" attitude, making the best of the situation.

Linsey watched Cade hobble around the yard on the walking cast he'd had for a day. In the tradition of his hero, he'd never complained in all the weeks he'd worn the metal contraption, more like scaffolding than a brace. But Linsey knew that the sheer weight of it, along with the awkwardness of a knee not allowed to bend, had worn him down. So now he viewed the clumsy cast that encased his foot but stopped short of his knee as a welcome change. Progress within limits. But progress of any degree was to be cherished.

With an exuberant smile on his face he could hardly sit still long enough to finish his breakfast this morning. When she said he might be excused, he'd bounded out of his chair ready to begin the day. Discovering Lincoln had been called out before dawn and hadn't returned brought the single shadow to Cade's smile. But even missing the tall, dark man who had made such a difference in his life hadn't dimmed his joy completely.

With Brownie as his shadow, Cade had spent the day revisiting and exploring the clearing and even the creek. The latter had given Linsey pause, though she knew the Cades had worked as teams, two brothers to a bank, walking more than a mile each direction, making sure no other dangers lurked near the stream. Remembering four men, who were like no men she'd ever known, inspecting rocks and bushes so thoroughly one could believe this was the most important factor in their lives, Linsey hadn't called out the instinctive warning. On this special day she would not remind Cade of another day of fear and pain.

It had taken weeks for the wound to heal and the metal brace to come off. The next step in the healing process was the cast. It was heavy and unwieldy, but to Cade it represented freedom. Not quite the freedom he wanted. But, as he'd told her while she tucked him into bed the night before, he would be okay. This was when she first heard her son embrace the code of all the Cades. She knew it wouldn't be the last.

"Make the best of the situation. Is that what Lincoln's doing now?" He'd proven himself a concerned, involved father and, when the rare opportunity arose, an attentive suitor and lover. But was it for real? Linsey didn't know. She'd lost all perspective long ago.

How could she fault a man who was there for both Stuarts night and day? A week after Cade had come home from the hospital, Lincoln resumed his practice of veterinary medicine, dividing his day into four parts. Beginning first with them, second with the practice, third came chores Belle Reve and Gus Cade demanded of his sons. What should have been an exhausting day ended as it began, with the Stuarts. A killing pace, but Lincoln never seemed tired. He never complained.

Haley Garrett took up what slack he would allow, and his brothers joined forces to help. Through it all Linsey was in limbo. Though there had been nights when Cade was asleep and resting comfortably that Lincoln had enticed her to the tack room, then made passionate love to her, she still had no idea where this was truly heading. No inkling how it would end for her.

Yet, when he smiled and teased, beguiling her with sweet kisses and naughty caresses, she couldn't refuse him. When she fretted over being too faraway to hear Cade's call should he need her, her wickedly determined lover became a caring father who understood that only the power of a mother's deep concern could be stronger than desire. As quickly as a frown could turn to a smile a monitor was installed between Cade's room and the barn.

Cade loved it. Lincoln encouraged him to speak to him any hour of the night. And he had. Many evenings as Linsey finished her chores after Cade's bedtime, she would pause to listen to the indistinct whispering of a boy speaking of his dreams to the man he loved with all his might.

It was the sort of gesture Linsey had come to expect from Lincoln. Another kindness that drew her deeper under his spell, Perhaps she was in limbo with no solid footing. But what did footing matter when one was walking on air?

Lincoln was tender and attentive. He beguiled and bewitched, drawing her to him with kisses and soft whispers, time and again. And each time was like it was the first time. Though in these weeks he'd learned to know her body and her needs better than she—where to touch, where to kiss, when to stroke, when to suckle, when to withdraw until she went mad for want of him—each time was new, fresh, wild. Making love with Lincoln was like an addictive psychedelic that offered ever-changing fantasies.

He was friend, mentor, champion, the family she'd never had. He was tough and kind, strong and tender. He was power and grace, fire and ice, thunder and lightning. He'd loved her in the heat of the storm and in cooling darkness. Then he had danced with her in morning rain and made her believe she could be beautiful.

As she knelt in the garden, redolent with sunlight and the rich dark scent of newly turned soil, all she need do was close her eyes and she was in the dark shadowy barn. Her fingers tingled with the memory of the feel of him. The sleek lines of his body, the tensing coiled muscles. The taste, the texture, the slick, steamy heat of embracing bodies.

When she was with him, she didn't recognize the woman she became. The wanton who felt things, knew things, did things neither plain Linsey Blair nor Linsey Stuart ever could. All for Lincoln, splendid, magnificent, naked...

"Mom?"

Linsey opened dreamy, unfocused eyes.

"Mom, are you okay?" Cade stood at the garden gate. Brownie, as always, at his side.

"Sure. I was just resting." She smiled at Cade. "How about you? Having a good time with Brownie?"

"Yep. But I got a problem." Cade's hands spread wide to demonstrate. "A big, big, big problem."

Linsey was instantly alert, the drowsy reminiscence gone like a morning mist burned away by the sun. Abruptly rising, she moved to the garden gate, fumbling for the latch but, in her fear, couldn't find it. "Did you trip? Have you hurt your leg?"

"Naw, Mom." Cade hung his head. For once he didn't wear the recovered Stetson. "I'm sorry, I didn't mean to scare you."

"Don't be sorry, tiger." Lincoln materialized out of no-where, scooping the boy into his arms. "It's a mother's God-given prerogative to worry."

"A dad's, too?" Cade was nose-to-nose with Lincoln, his forehead tilting the brim of the second-best hat.

"Yep," Lincoln assured him. "A dad's, too."

"Did *you* worry when I trapped my leg?" Cade was solemn, his eyes crinkled in avid regard, holding Lincoln's.

"Did I worry?" Lincoln assumed a look of exaggerated shock. "Oh boy, did I! More than anybody in the whole world, except your mom."

"I dunno." Cade's face screwed into a frown, his attention riveted on Lincoln. "Jefferson was awful worried."

"That's true, he was," Lincoln agreed. "In fact, every-body was worried. Adams, Jackson, Eden, Cullen, Jesse. Even old Gus Cade was worried when he heard about it. But you can bet your bottom dollar no one was as worried as your mom and me. No sir."

Cade shook his head sorrowfully. "I ain't got a dollar. Bottom or top. Does that change it?"

"Nothing changes it, Cade. Nothing can. Not ever."

Cade nodded then, satisfied with Lincoln's assurances.

Linsey curbed her emotions as unobtrusively as she could. When it came to Cade and Lincoln, she was like a brimming watering pot, always spilling over. She knew what Cade was asking, what he was hoping. A man as sensitive as Lincoln would know, as well.

*Where do we go from here?* she wondered in the silence that fell over the garden.

"Jefferson said I got your blood." Cade twisted a button on Lincoln's shirt, staring at it as if he needed someplace safe to look. "When I asked why the doctors didn't just get some from that bank like they did for Lucky, he said it was 'cause the bank didn't have the kind that would work for me."

"Jefferson's right. You needed blood. The problem was that yours is a special kind of blood. The bank didn't have any and neither do many people."

"Not even Mom? Even though I came out of her tummy?"

"No, tiger, your mom doesn't have the same kind of blood you have." Lincoln's gaze met Linsey's over Cade's head as, softly, he added, "Even though you came out of her tummy."

"But you do?" Cade leaned back in Lincoln's arms, his questioning, silver gaze lifting to meet Lincoln's.

"That's right, I do." Lincoln nodded, and his gaze was shaded again, by the brim of his hat. "You only needed a little, but I would have given all I had if that little wasn't enough."

"Would Lucky's work, if he was here instead of in the ground in Oregon?"

"No, Cade." Lincoln's half smile was sad. "Lucky's wouldn't have worked."

"So we got the same kind of blood. Almost just us. 'Cept now it's mixed in me." Cade returned his attention to the button. "Does that mean we're blood brothers, or somethin'?" Small shoulders lifted beneath a worn shirt. "Like in the movies when Indians adopt somebody."

Lincoln glanced at Linsey, standing amid a row of flowers. He found no help there. She was as surprised by this turn of Cade's interest as he. Lincoln was on his own, with only instinct to guide him. Right or wrong, instinct warned he must be truthful and not burden the boy with more than he was asking.

"We won't be brothers, exactly," Lincoln answered at last. "But that's close enough for now."

Cade accepted the explanation. But neither Linsey nor Lincoln doubted that, after he pondered awhile, he would need more to satisfy an intense curiosity.

Lincoln set the boy down carefully. "You told your mom you had a problem. Want to tell me about it?"

"It's the colt."

"The one you were supposed to name?" Lincoln asked.

"Yes, sir. 'Cept I haven't yet, 'cause I couldn't think of anythin' good till now."

Linsey stepped closer. Over the garden fence she brushed back the shock of brown hair that had fallen over Cade's forehead. "But you have a name now?"

"Not exactly, Mom. And Jesse says it's long, long, long past time the little rascal knew who he was."

"You didn't know what to call him before, but you have an idea now, right?" Lincoln suspected he knew where Cade was going with this, and it couldn't be better for his plan.

"First I thought the bestest name was Diablo, like Lincoln's horse. Then I figgered that might not be so good. If I called him, it might scare him if the real Diablo came, too."

Cade was an unconscious mimic. Linsey heard a mix of Jesse Lee's cowboy idioms and the lowcountry drawl of all the Cades. His mannerisms were pure Lincoln. "What have you decided?"

"I still dunno, Mom." Cade turned a deadly serious gaze to his mother. "But since I'm a blood brother, at least kinda, I thought maybe an Indian name. 'Cept I don't know any."

"I know someone who does," Lincoln said too casually.

"Who, Lincoln? Who?" The boy was practically dancing, cast and all, in his excitement.

Linsey felt like a forgotten intruder as she watched the two men in her life. But she didn't feel neglected. This was how she would want it to be between them, if...

"If that's all right." Lincoln's tone was gently questioning. "Is it, Linsey?"

"I beg your pardon?" Frowning, she was aware she'd plainly missed some critical issue. "Is what all right?"

"Lincoln says Jefferson's going to camp out with Merrie in his tree house and I can go, too. If you say it's okay. If I can, Jefferson can name me some good names for the colt."

"Whoa." Palms outstretched, Linsey signaled a halt. "I missed something here. Jefferson's camping out in a tree house?"

"That's right," Lincoln answered. "He started it when he was a kid and has built on it for years. Now it's rather like the Swiss Family Robinson revisited."

"Who's the Swiss family?" Cade piped in.

"Never mind, Cade," Linsey muttered grimly. "I'll tell you later." To Lincoln she said, "Jefferson, Merrie and Cade in a tree all night? I don't think so."

"It isn't like you think."

Linsey cut him off. "How do you know what I'm thinking?"

"Considering your behavior the past few weeks, sweetheart, it isn't hard. And to tell the truth, it's kinda nice to know your mind turns to that so easily."

"Lincoln," she scolded. "How dare you?"

"Oh, I dare a lot of things when you're concerned, sweetheart." He was grinning when he began, but now he was sober. "There's nothing to be concerned about. Jefferson and Merrie are no more than hunting and fishing and riding buddies. Jefferson's damned nigh celibate, and Merrie's so innocent that if any creature but a horse kissed her, she would scrub her own mouth out with soap."

"You can't know that." Trowel in hand, unmindful of the dirt clinging to it, Linsey crossed her arms over her breasts.

"I do, love. Women trail after Jefferson, but he doesn't

notice. Men fall over their own feet over Merrie. If they aren't on horseback, she doesn't know they're alive. They're a couple of overgrown kids, one afraid of relationships, the other not ready. Instead they're best friends—as Lucky and I were.''

He waited until that little reminder sank in, then continued. ''They've asked if Cade could go. It would do the boy no harm, and both of them would look after him and protect him with their lives. The tree house is more like a leafy castle than anything. It would be the adventure of a lifetime.'' His look dared her to disappoint the boy. ''The decision is ultimately yours.''

''Please, Mom. I never slept in a tree house.'' Cade looked across the fence, a hopeful expression on his face. ''The colt needs a name, and it was Jefferson who worked on a ranch. Jefferson and Jesse. But Jesse says he's stumped. Bad stumped.''

The real implications of the heated conversation had flown over Cade's head. For that Linsey was grateful. But not for Lincoln's methods. ''You sandbagged me.''

''What's sandbag?'' Cade piped in.

''I didn't.'' Lincoln's look of innocence couldn't fool a fool, much less Linsey. ''Like Cade said, the colt needs a name, an Indian name from a blood brother. What better source than Jeffie?''

''Cade doesn't need to spend the night in a tree.''

''Yes, he does. It's an experience he won't forget.''

''He could fall out.''

''He isn't going to fall out of anything. The boy's so surefooted sometimes I think he's a cat.''

''His cast.''

''He's wearing a cast, so what? He'll be surefooted with one foot and sure-casted with the other.''

Linsey ignored Cade's giggle, but Lincoln's answering smile turned irritation to anger. ''What if it rains?''

''The tree house has a thatched roof. Merrie and Jefferson and Cade would be dry.'' A slow, sly smile tilted wickedly handsome lips. ''But we could dance.''

Linsey was shocked into silence. The memory of Lincoln wearing only low-slung jeans, dancing in a sunlit morning mist, stole her breath away.

''His cast shouldn't...shouldn't get wet,'' she stuttered in repetition because she could think of nothing else to say.

''Jefferson's had casts, and Merrie, too. So they both know how to treat one. Anyway, Cade's not only sure-footed, he's too smart to fall out of a tree.'' Lincoln ruffled Cade's dark hair, then let his hand slide down to the boyish nape where it grew in the same swirling pattern as his own. ''Right, tiger?''

''Yes, sir.'' Cade's head had turned back and forth keeping track of this repartee. Now he added his own plea again. ''Please, Mom. I'll be good and do exactly what Jefferson and Merrie say.''

''I...I don't know.'' Linsey was clearly vacillating, her adamant stance weakening. ''I'll have to think about it.''

''Better think fast,'' Lincoln warned. ''The tree dwellers have arrived.''

''You planned this,'' she accused, and glared at Lincoln as Cade scampered off to greet the new arrivals.

''Not really, but I wish I had.'' Reaching over the fence to take her hand, he held her gaze. ''Cade will enjoy himself. I guarantee they'll take good care of him. And you, my love? You need a change of scenery and a change of pace.''

''What pace? What scenery?'' she asked in sudden weariness as Brownie began to bark a greeting.

''Don't worry. We'll take good care of him. I promise.'' From his place by the opposite side of Jefferson's battered Land Rover, Lincoln heard Merrie Alexandre's soft, encouraging words, delivered in a calm and pleasing contralto that would instill confidence in the most doubtful. In the course of two years under Eden's tutelage, he'd watched her grow from a frightened, homesick, resentful child, to an excitable young girl discovering her way and the way of the new world into which her father had thrust her in his determination to make a lady of her. Finally, with surprising speed, the child and young girl had metamorphosed into the stunning, assured young woman who smiled at Linsey as they waited for Cade and Brownie.

Marissa Claire Alexandre was stunning, accomplished, and frighteningly intelligent. But she was unaware of the effect of her calm manner. And of her striking looks, with rich-brown hair falling straight from her crown, then curling at the tips as it brushed her waist. With eyes as dark, the slender, long-legged beauty hadn't a clue what earthy dreams she inspired in the young bucks of Belle Terre. And some not so young.

"Got 'em." Cade spoke of Lincoln's first best hat sitting at a rakish angle over his right eye, and of the book of horses Lincoln had given him. "Merrie's gonna read to me."

"From what Lincoln tells me, you can recite it to Merrie and me." Jefferson bent over Cade, flashing his hundred-watt smile at the boy as he took the book. "When we come back, you'll have a couple of names to try out on the colt. Maybe we'll think of some extraspecial good names while we watch the stars."

"In the dark?" Cade's eyes were shining even more at the prospect of staying up late.

"Sure." Jefferson laughed, a low, musical note Linsey rarely heard. "You know any other time to watch stars?" He handed the book to Merrie, tossed Cade's knapsack in the truck and coaxed Brownie into the back. Then he swooped the boy up in his arms. "So, tiger, give your beautiful mom a kiss."

He leaned forward to let Cade kiss her, then dropped one of his own on her forehead, saying for Linsey, alone, "To quote Marissa Claire, don't worry. We'll take good care of him. That's a promise straight from the heart.''

Turning away with a flourish, he sat Cade in the truck, tipped the hat down even lower, saying in a tough-guy voice, "This is the shotgun seat, so keep your eyes peeled, pardner.''

Cade was still laughing and Merrie was settled in when Jefferson climbed in himself. The engine was running, the truck in gear and ready. "Quite a lady," he said too softly for Linsey to hear as Merrie engaged her in another assuring conversation. "Quite a boy.''

"I know." As strong, callused hands slid over shirtsleeves to clasp forearms in the brotherly salute of affection, Lincoln added, "I've known for a long time.''

"It's time." Hands fell away. Jefferson gripped the steering wheel as he studied his brother's face. "Past time.''

"To stake my claim and tell the world they're mine?''

"If you've got a lick of sense.''

"It isn't that easy, Jeffie." Lincoln's face turned grim. "There were other things to consider. Other things than my own feelings and what I want.''

"There's a time to be the pragmatic stoic, and times to be the impetuous lover who reaches out in secret to take what he can't resist. But there comes a time, even for you, when that isn't enough. Any fool can see that time is now." Jefferson lifted his foot from the brake, and the truck gathered speed. But not so much that Lincoln didn't hear his parting shot. "Now! Brother.''

"That seemed pretty serious. What was that all about?'' Linsey watched the truck ford the stream and disappear.

"Jeffie was just giving some stern advice.''

"Stern advice? Jefferson?" Linsey cast a look of surprise at Lincoln. "I didn't think Jefferson ever presumed to meddle.''

"He doesn't." Lincoln looped an arm over her shoulders. "Except in dire cases of blind stupidity.''

Linsey laughed, not quite as uninhibited by concern for Cade's adventure as he would like, but a sound Lincoln loved. "I've never known you to be blind or stupid."

"Jeffie's right, I have been this time." As he walked with her to the house, he said almost to himself, "But no more."

Spinning her from the shelter of his arms, he caught her hands in his. "That's something to think of later. At the moment I have plans for you. I hope they meet your approval."

"What plans?"

"A night away from the farm." When she would have demurred, Lincoln silenced her with a kiss. "Jefferson knows I keep my beeper with me. He knows the number, and he won't hesitate to call. Brownie's gone, the house is clean, the barn is empty. Best of all, Cade's having the adventure of his life. And," he added in mock severity, "if you come up with any other excuse, I assure you, I will have a valid argument against it."

"Uh-huh," Linsey agreed. "That's why I'm not arguing."

"It's a smart lady who knows a determined man when she sees one." Glancing at the sun that had begun to dip behind tall trees, he planned his schedule. "I need to run over to Belle Reve, check in on Gus and Jesse. That should take no more than an hour. Will that give you time enough to get ready?"

"If I knew where we're going, I would know how to dress."

"Where we're going is a surprise." Threading his fingers through tendrils that had made their usual escape from the band at her nape, he tucked them behind her ear. "Dress for your mood." His smile made scandalous promises. "This is a special night. One to make of what you wish. Let that be your guide."

"In an hour." Her voice was unsteady in response to the thrill of her pulse.

"An hour," he promised. Dropping one last kiss on her waiting lips, he turned her toward the Stuart farmhouse.

"This is amazing." Linsey wandered the courtyard garden where gaslights cast fanciful shadows on a rectangle of lush grass bordered by magnificent shrubs and exotic flowers. "So simple. So unexpected. No stranger to Belle Terre would ever imagine that at the end of a narrow cul-de-sac, behind these old brick walls and the ancient gate, lies a tiny paradise."

"I wouldn't be so rash as to call it paradise." Lincoln chuckled. "But it's my home, when I have time for it."

"Time," Linsey paused by a heavy-headed gardenia of pale cream, cupping it in her palm, delighting in its velvet texture. "You've had very little in the last months." Releasing the bloom, she turned to him. "I'm sorry."

"Don't be." Lincoln stood in the shadows, watching her. Her hair had been drawn up in a mass of curls at her nape, but had begun the inevitable drift to her shoulders. She wore a gown of aged, delicate cream. One of Frannie's treasures from her uninhibited youth. The Stuart rebel had been taller, heavier of bone, but with fabric so soft and supple it didn't matter. As it fluttered over the top of Linsey's instep and swayed around her body, no dress could have been more alluring or more perfect. "Don't be sorry. I spent the time as I wished, with whom I wished."

Moving to her, he snapped the stem of the gardenia and tucked it into the cleft of the décolletage of her borrowed gown. "A lovely token for an even lovelier lady."

"Thank you." Her fingertips brushed fragrant petals.

"No arguments?" He caught straying fingers in his.

"You make me believe, Lincoln. Only you." She couldn't look away from his gaze, couldn't get enough of him.

Bringing her hand to his lips, he kissed each fingertip. "I watched Merrie with you today. It struck me how alike you are, in that neither of you knows yet who you are. Neither of you understands or reckons with your own power."

"I'm nothing like Merrie. She's the most…"

Lincoln ignored her denial. "You don't understand, not by a long shot. But you will." His arms closed around her as he bent to her. An instant before his mouth took her waiting, parted lips, he muttered, "Before this night is done, before *I* am done, you will, my love. You will."

# Eleven

He had called her "love" before. But never with that tender note of possession. Never with the look that made her feel as if she had stepped into a warm cocoon where nothing had gone before. A place where guilt didn't exist, nor worry, nor regret. Here in a small, walled garden, there was only Lincoln and the promise of enchantment she saw in his smile, felt in his touch.

His fingers twining into hers, he led her along a winding path where light and shadow gathered in ever-changing layers. Where gaslights blended with moonlight painting foliage and fragile blossoms in pale gold and cool silver. Moving past their glow, he went with her beneath an ancient myrtle with gnarled branches reaching in twisted ribbons toward the star-studded sky. Darkness ruled for a little while, becoming black velvet with a glittering edge of gray. Beyond the circle of the tree, beyond the reach of gaslights, bathed only in moonlight rose a spiraling staircase leading to the bedroom of Lincoln's antebellum home.

Here the garden was even lovelier. In the days when the
house was constructed, it would have been a kitchen garden
supplying fresh vegetables and fruits, rather than flowers.
Now it was the most secluded and charming facet of a
private sanctuary. Etched in the shimmering light of only
the moon, it was an enchanted bower. A place for lovers.

"It's perfect," she whispered. "A world set apart."

"There's more," Lincoln promised as with a slight tug
he led her up the winding stairs. Even the clatter of their
footsteps on metal seemed like music in the night. This
enchanted night.

"Look." Lincoln stood at the edge of the balcony, a
sweep of his free hand offering all of Belle Terre and the
glittering river beyond for her enjoyment alone.

From this vantage point, the garden seemed surreal, a
glorious dream. The city and the river beyond the wall were
from another life. One suspended in this small moment.
"This is what you come home to at the end of weary
days."

"When I can."

Linsey turned from the railing, from the garden to Lincoln, who was her dream and her reality. "It's beautiful."

"Yes," he said simply. "But never as beautiful as you."

Linsey didn't demur or respond. But when he tugged
gently at her hand, she went with him to a narrow bench
where he sat before her. His head tilted, his gaze searching,
he looked up at her. Lincoln, breaking his own rule, sitting
when a lady stood.

A rare moment. A rare vantage as the awareness that lay
beneath the surface trembled between them. In moonlight
his dark hair became diamond-tipped ebony. As she lifted
a hand to stroke the shining mane, he caught her palm,
keeping it against his cheek, turning his mouth into the
sensitive hollow.

She felt the warm stroke of his tongue, and her body
shuddered in anticipation. When he released her and his

hands settled on her hips to bring her into the space between his bent legs, she went willingly. In that intimate
proximity, yet not touching, a slow heat began to burn deep
and low within her in answer to his whispered promise.
"Beginning now I'm going to let you see just how beautiful
you are."

His hands still lying lightly on her hips began to move
in gliding caresses up her midriff and over her breasts. She
was naked under the flowing fabric, he had known that and
been maddened by the bold provocation. Now as her
breasts filled his hands, the nipples like pearls beneath the
circling stroke of his thumbs, he knew he'd never encoun-
tered anything as seductive as Linsey naked beneath the
delicate veil of aged silk.

"You were ready for this." His palms cupped her
breasts, and he watched again how perfectly their softness
fit him.

As his thumbs circled and circled, Linsey braced against
his shoulders. "I saw this in your eyes. As I dressed, I
hoped."

Lincoln leaned forward to follow with his tongue the
path his thumbs had taken. Then moved away to admire
the look of silk clinging to the moisture of his caress. "You
didn't hope, Linsey." His gaze lifted to hold hers. "From
the first day, you knew it would be like this between us.
You always knew."

"Yes," she whispered as he embraced her. When his
lips closed over the crest of her breast, into the welcome
ache she spoke a truth she hadn't faced. "I knew." Her
fingers threaded through his hair, cradling him to her. "I
hoped," she repeated the litany as she offered her body to
him. "I was afraid, yet I knew."

His suckling changed from hot and hard to sweet and
slow. Languid tugs with the curl of his tongue sent shards
of escalating desire lancing through her. When she was sure
she couldn't endure any more, he lifted his head again.

"I wanted to do this the night of the wind storm, when I brought Eden's wine to your bath. I wanted it more than I'd ever wanted anything in my life. You were ravishing, with a bubble here." The stroke of his tongue over her sensitized nipple nearly brought her to her knees, but he was too intent on his maddening dialogue to notice. "And a bubble here."

The demonstrative remembrance went on. Linsey wanted him to stop. She feared he would. When she was nearly mindless, sure she could stand no more, his hands skimmed down her body past her hips and her thighs, to the hem of her dress. Gradually he raised the filmy cloth and, as gradually, kissed his way up her body. Rising to her breasts again, he halted for one more kiss, one more caress, before he muttered his hoarse demand. "Take it off."

Linsey didn't demur or hesitate. After all, seeking the perfect gown for the perfect night, she had searched through Frannie Stuart's clothing packed so carefully away in heavy trunks. When she'd despaired that there could be such a garment, she'd discovered the gown she wore. A cherished treasure, folded away with loving care, aged, faded, but still elegant. Certain it held special memories, perhaps beloved secrets, she'd dressed in anticipation of this moment. A moment she, too, would remember forever—when the gown lay discarded at her feet and she would be naked beneath Lincoln's gaze and his touch.

The evening, begun with dinner neither had eaten and wine neither had drunk, was never meant to be more than this. Pretenses at social conventions had merely been tantalizing foreplay. Destiny had arrived. Slowly Linsey crossed her arms over her breasts as she clutched the rippled hem of borrowed finery. On held breath, her single garment fluttered to the balcony floor.

Lincoln was silent. Linsey waited. In the luster of the moon she saw celebration of the gifts she brought him. His groan was guttural and harsh with controlled need. "I said you were beautiful. Until now, even I didn't realize how very beautiful.''

Before she would react to the compliment, he was catching her hands bringing them to his lean hard body. ''Your turn.''

Linsey needed no other invitation. Emboldened by courage he provoked and confidence he instilled, driven by her own desire, she began the leisurely seduction of undressing this virile, much-loved, handsome man. He had promised that before this night was done she would believe she was beautiful. In return, Linsey vowed that before this sweet interlude was through, Lincoln Cade would know there was no other woman on the earth for him.

She began with his watch. When his eyes widened, she laughed, ''Cade's with Jefferson, Haley's taking barn call. Everyone else has the horses and Gus under control. We have nowhere to be until sunrise, so who cares what time it is or isn't?''

Lincoln laughed with her, committing to memory this rare woman. He watched moonlight sculpt shapely curves in silver and shadow. With her hair wild about her shoulders, she might have been a nymph come to drink from the fountain and sleep beneath the flowers. She might have been. But he was immeasurably grateful this nymph was flesh and blood, and his. At least for the night.

In this newfound confidence and a not-so-innocent tease, Linsey let her fingers trail across his shoulder and down his chest to the snap at the waist of his trousers. When he caught a breath just short of a groan, she laughed and slipped her hands over his midriff, then his chest and his throat. He'd dressed in casual chic. But it was simply as Lincoln would dress for the occasion. As he would dress for her.

His shirt was pristine white, of a fabric that emulated heavy silk. The feel of it gliding over his skin and beneath her palms was sensual and utterly sinful. She liked to touch him, she liked the sensation of his heated skin beneath the fabric. And in her pleasure she touched, explored, caressed, and adored.

Lincoln's body was taut, a sheen of moisture gathered on his forehead as he struggled for control. When he thought the seat of the narrow bench would break beneath his grip, she slipped the first button free. Then the second, and the third. When the last was done, it was Lincoln who cast it away. The cool night air soothed him, but in the lurch of a racing heart he discovered that if her touch through the barrier of fabric was maddening, the glide of her bare hands over his body defied description.

But Linsey the tormentor was as caught as he in this trap of her own making. And it was Linsey who, with a cry, captured his hands in hers to bring him to his feet. Snaps unsnapped, the rasp of a zipper joined the quiet sound of the splashing fountain. "Now," she cried as tailored trousers were tossed aside and he stood before her, proudly male, wanting her. "Now."

"Yes." He lifted her from her feet, then took her down with him to the small bench. Settling her across him, he joined with her in gentle degrees, cradling her body with his until she took him completely. Together they moved. With each touch of her breasts against his chest he savored her acceptance. When he would have been careful, letting her set an easy pace, it was Linsey whose body arched. Linsey who demanded more. Linsey who would have him irrevocably, without caution until both were spent.

With his body Lincoln answered. Then they were moving like music. Like the sweep of tides. Like everything beautiful either had ever known. "Look at me, Linsey," he whispered in the hushed rhythm. "Look into my eyes and know how much I adore you. See your power and believe how beautiful you are."

She did see. She did believe that in his eyes she was beautiful. In his gift of words, sweet, wild torment flowed into the even sweeter ecstasy of the storm before the calm. When the wonder was done, spent and quiet, she went into the shelter of his embrace. For longer than she could fathom, he held her. For longer than either cared they watched the night, one as awestruck as the other, as exhausted, as incurably, unalterably in love.

At their feet the garden lay still, with the fountain catching moonbeams as if it were midday and it was the sun it caught. Into the quiet intruded the rumble of carriage wheels and the steady drum of tired horses' hooves striking the pavement. In the darkness the driver soothed his weary steeds in a singsong voice, explaining their shift was almost done.

As gradually as it began, the small intrusion faded. The balcony with ashen light spilling over two spent lovers, was as quiet as before. Until Lincoln clasped her tighter. Sensing a strange urgency, Linsey lifted a questioning gaze to his. Lincoln dropped a lingering kiss on her upturned mouth. "It was nothing," he said in a gruff tone. "Nothing, except that I love you."

Then she was swept from her feet as he took her to his bed. Where he promised to make love to her through the remaining hours of the night.

Lincoln woke at sunrise. As she had when they made love in the tack room, Linsey stood by the balcony door, barefoot and naked beneath his open shirt. "It looks better on you."

"Lincoln." She spun to face him in the bright glow of morning. "I didn't mean to wake you."

"You didn't, except by your absence. But, to risk repeating myself, I like your choice of attire."

"Thank you." She made a mock curtsy, gathering his shirt to her, reveling in the lingering scent of Lincoln.

"What were you looking at just now?" he asked. "What were you thinking?"

"I wanted to see the garden in daylight. I wondered if it could be as enchanting as it was in the night."

Lincoln had drawn the sheet around his hips, now he went very still, his gaze seeking hers. "And is it?"

Linsey was mesmerized by him. By his body, dark against the crisp, white sheet. By the heavy-lidded look of a sated lover. "Everything's as wonderful in the light as in the dark."

When her voice faded and she fell silent, he asked, "Then would you come live with me and be my love, my life?"

"Here?" Of the thousands of questions she would ask, this was the one to which she could give voice. "In Belle Terre?"

"Here. The farm. Oregon, if you wish. Anywhere."

"What about Cade?"

"I love Cade. He loves me. You heard him, the questions he asked, the assurance he was seeking. He wants a father. He wants that father to be me, and he's ready to hear the truth."

"You would tell him you're his father, not Lucky? How could you explain that to a child?"

"We'll answer whatever questions he asks, together. As time goes on, and he asks more, we'll answer those, as well."

"You said he should be allowed to decide who he will be. Stuart or Cade." Lincoln's confiscated shirt crumpled in her fists. "If he should choose Stuart, what then?"

"I hope he chooses Cade. If not, we'll manage."

"What will you tell the others?" The others—Lincoln's brothers, his father, his friends.

Throwing back the sheet, not caring that he was naked, he went to her. A finger at her chin tilted her face to his. "What will I tell them? The truth, to those who matter. Nothing to those who don't. I've said my brothers would never judge you. Nor, in a town with its share of scandals and skeletons, will anyone else.''

"Let the innocent cast the first stone? The theory being no one is without sin—thus, no stones.'' Linsey fought back a shudder. "We both know it isn't really like that.''

"Then we'll cope.''

"And Cade?''

"We'll teach him to cope, by instilling pride in who he is. Pride no one can take from him.''

"It shouldn't be this way.''

"In a perfect world, no. But our flawed world is the best we have.'' His arms closed harder around her. "Together we can make it as nearly perfect as it can be.''

"I took your child, Lincoln.''

"A child who for months you didn't know existed.'' With the back of his hand he stroked her throat. "If I hadn't called what occurred between us in the fire a mistake, if I hadn't turned away from you, would you have married Lucky?''

Linsey's gaze strayed over the garden, Lincoln's sanctuary. The home of a kind, generous man. One who would take the lion's share of guilt, if she would allow it. "It's done. Placing blame can't change it.''

"Answer my question. Look at me and tell me the truth. If you'd known I wanted you, little girl lost, would you have chosen Lucky, or me?''

"Lucky was sick, he needed me. I would have done almost anything to help.'' Now her eyes dulled with grief.

"Anything but marry him, if I hadn't been a fool,'' he finished for her.

"You were my first love, my only love. What I felt for Lucky was the love of a friend for a friend. That never changed. To my sorrow and Lucky's, I couldn't love him as he wanted to be loved, or as much as he deserved.''

"Then do what he would want now. He took my love and my child from me. Then spent years making reparations by teaching Cade about a grand and illustrious Lincoln Cade. At the end he asked my promise to help you, then sent you both to me. You couldn't love Lucky because you loved me. When he realized what his life was going to be, I don't think he minded.

"So, with his blessing and our own forgiveness, shall we make the best of a wonderful situation? Will you live with me and be my only love for the rest of our lives?"

Linsey stared into his clear gray eyes and saw love. "Yes." She rose to his kiss murmuring, "Oh, yes."

"Linsey." Her name was a low growl, breathed against her skin, as his body grew hard against her own. "You talk too much."


"Jefferson said a lot of Indians speak Spanish so we thought about Afortunada. Which means Lucky in Spanish, like Diablo means devil. But then, it might be shortened to Nada, which means nothin', and the colt for sure is somethin'. So we picked Hijo del Diablo, which means son of the devil. Then Jefferson said that sounded too much like cussin'. So the cussin' name will go on the colt's registering papers, but we'll just call him Sonny."

"Sounds like a good idea." Linsey kissed the top of Cade's head as she passed by the kitchen table where he sat, legs swinging, eyes dancing. "Is the colt Diablo's son?"

"Jefferson said he was."

*Jefferson said, Jefferson said.* Linsey wondered how many times she'd heard that phrase in the three days since Cade's tree house adventure. "Then Sonny will be a handsome fellow."

"Yep." Cade nodded. "Jefferson said if I trained him real good, Jackson would prob'ly let me keep him here at the farm."

"Ah, so the colt must be one of the Black Arabians."

"Of course he is, Mom. He's Hijo del Diablo."

Linsey laughed. "If you spend much more time with Jefferson, you'll be speaking Spanish like a Spaniard."

The sound of a galloping horse brought Cade from his chair. "Must be Merrie. She said she'd ride over from Grampa Gus's house and give me a ride back so's Miss Corey can keep me."

Linsey set down an unwashed dish. "Grampa Gus?"

"Sure." Cade snatched his hat from the rack and brushed away an imaginary speck of dust. "He said since my name is Cade, same as his, I could pretend I'm his grandboy and he's my grampa."

No one had guessed the truth and told Cade before she or Lincoln could. In relief she tried a smile. "Grandboy? Well, that's good. I suppose."

"Jefferson and Jesse said it was good. Partic'ly since Old Gus is a son of a pirate. Mom? Do you 'spose he wore a patch over his eye? The pirate, I mean."

"I don't know, tiger." Wondering what pirates had to do with anything, Linsey went to answer Merrie's knock. "Why don't you see what Jefferson says."

Minutes later she was on the porch waving goodbye to Cade and Merrie and wondering if this night was a mistake. But she had no time to ponder, for Lincoln would be arriving shortly to take her to dinner at The Inn at River Walk. Where they would be joined by Adams and Eden, Jackson and Jefferson. Before the night was done, the entire Cade clan, with the exception of Gus Cade, would have their suspicions of her son's parentage confirmed.

Even short on time, she watched the huge black horse, the pretty Argentinean and Cade until they faded from sight.

She was barely ready when Lincoln knocked. Turning before the mirror, she studied the gown she'd spent much of her savings on in Belle Terre. "Okay, but not great. In for a penny, in for a pound. Soon I have to get a job."

"Why?"

"Lincoln! You startled me. Why knock if you're going to come right in?"

"Why is the door unlocked if you didn't want me to? And what the hell is this folderol about getting a job?" he demanded, glaring at her from her bedroom doorway.

Lincoln had decreed the evening must be an occasion. He'd dressed accordingly in black tux, black tie, tucked shirt and navy brocade vest. He was more handsome than sin, but Linsey tried not to see. Tonight she needed to keep her wits about her. "It's nothing you should be concerned with." Hoping he would accept this dismissal, she scanned the room. "My purse?"

"Your purse is here." He took it from a chair by the door. "I like your gown, by the way. Lavender becomes you." Laying her purse in her outstretched hands, he regarded her with an obdurate expression. "Explain the job."

Linsey had hoped to avoid this conversation until the job was fact. "I'm applying for a position with the ranger station."

"Why?"

"Because I need to work. I would have applied long before now, if it weren't for Cade's accident."

"You don't need to work."

"But I do." Carefully she kept her anxiety from her tone. "We have no income but plenty of bills. Particularly hospital and surgeon's fees."

"That's my responsibility. As for the rest, if you insist on independence, you have Jackson's rent and timber to cut."

"No horses are stabled and pastured here yet. The timber isn't cut." Gathering up a wrap she would not need in the sultry night, she faced him. "Shall we continue to argue or go?"

Lincoln chuckled. "For a minute there, I forgot what an independent wench you are. We aren't going to argue, but it would be fun to kiss and make up. Especially since I brought a present.''

Linsey laughed as she went into his arms. She couldn't stay angry when he was so much like Cade at his contrite best. ''So?'' Leaning back, she looked up at him. ''About this present.''

''It's there on the table.''

She turned in the circle of his arms. ''A cup. One like Frannie's broken cup. Where did you find it?''

''There were several sets and parts of sets of china in the house in Belle Terre when I bought it. This is from a part. Don't say you can't take it, for we don't have time for another argument. Just thank me nicely with a kiss, then we can go.''

Linsey was laughing again, as he intended, when their lips met and clung for a long time.


''This is The Inn at River Walk?'' Linsey exclaimed as Lincoln opened the door of his sleek Jaguar for her.

Lincoln had told her the history of the majestic building that had belonged to Eden's family for centuries. This, and the other antebellum homes along the street, had been built for the mistresses of wealthy men, and the second families the relationships produced. The name of the street, Fancy Row, described the ladies and the style in which they lived.

''Originally it was just River Walk,'' he explained. ''After its heyday, it became a derelict, serving as storage for the trash and treasures of Eden's family.''

Linsey stood on the walk, staring up at the lovely home. ''Whoever the mistress was, she lived in style.''

''Keeping a mistress was an accepted practice. At its height, Fancy Row boasted the finest houses in Belle Terre. At its worst it became a slum.''

''Until Eden restored it. Now Adams has continued her mission, saving the rest of the homes on Fancy Row.''

''Exactly.'' As the valet parked the Jag, Lincoln took her

arm. Though he'd hoped the informative small talk would calm her, he felt her tremble. "Don't be nervous. No one is here to judge."

"I know, Lincoln. But knowing doesn't make it easier."

"Well la-de-da. Look who's here." A massive, unkempt man stepped out of the twilight shade of a tree, blocking their way.

"Rabb! What the hell are you doing here? Adams and Cullen will kill you if they catch you or any of your family within a mile of Eden. That is, if I don't do it first." Lincoln was livid. His grip on Linsey's arm painful. "I don't know what you want, but forget it. Leave now, while you still can."

"Oh, I going. But not before I get a look at the little lady." Beneath greasy black hair, eyes as black settled on Linsey. The stare probing her body made her feel unclean.

"So this is the one. I heard your whore had come to town, dragging your by-blow—"

Lincoln's vicious backhand slashing across his mouth sent the creature reeling. A smashed and bloody mouth silenced him, except for animal grunts as he charged Lincoln, head down, eyes blazing. The rest was a blur, peppered with soggy sounds of savage body blows and the thud of bone striking bone.

Before Linsey could react, it was finished. The man called Rabb scrabbled across the ground, while Lincoln stood over him, fists still clenched, eyes as cold as death. "That's right, Snake, crawl away and hide in the hole you came from. But if you or any other of your inbred family come within speaking distance of my wife and son, I'll find you and kill you."

Snake Rabb staggered to his feet, swaying like a hulking bear, hate burning in his eyes. As the door to the Inn burst open and Adams and Jackson and Jefferson were there with Cullen at their heels, he melted into the shadows again.

"Let him go," Lincoln said to his brothers. "Don't soil your hands with worthless filth."

"From the look of your hands, you're one to talk." Eden stepped calmly into the midst of the angry Cades. "But he's right." She slipped an arm around Linsey's waist. "No Rabb is worth the effort this feud requires, or the injury it inflicts."

With that, she led Linsey into the Inn. Such was the gentle strength of Eden Cade that the brothers followed like recalcitrant but obedient boys.

"I can't do this, Eden." Linsey sat by a window, staring at the river. "I don't care what bad blood lies between the Cades and Rabbs. I don't care if it's a feud of long standing and Cade was only an excuse. I can't expose him to the ugliness."

"What will you do?" Eden had seen to Lincoln's injuries, then had taken Linsey away while he spoke with Jericho Rivers, the sheriff of Belle Terre.

"For now, go back to the farm. As soon as I find a job, Cade and I will leave the lowcountry."

"You would take Lincoln's son from him?"

"To protect him. To protect both of them, yes." Neither considered that Lincoln would stop her or fight to take Cade from her. They both knew him too well.

"I wish I could make you understand this was an isolated incident, and really nothing to do with you or Cade."

"We were the catalyst," Linsey said bitterly. "One that could be used again to hurt all of you. But in the end, the greatest hurt would be Cade's."

"You're wrong. Cade's tougher than you realize." Rising, Eden looked down at the woman she knew was Lincoln's only love. "It isn't my place to persuade you to stay. But I hope you will. For Cade, for Lincoln…most of all, for yourself."

"I can't." Linsey looked away. "I won't."

"We'll see," Eden said. "Who knows who, or what, might change your mind? Lincoln will be a while with Jericho, but if you're determined to return to the farm, Cullen will take you."

At the door Eden turned back. "Just two more things before I go. First, one of the Rabbs took Adams from me for a long time. Don't let it happen again. Second, it's common knowledge that Noelle was conceived before Adams and I were married. Would you condemn me for it? I don't believe so. Neither has anyone else who matters. Think, Linsey. Think long and hard before you make a decision that could be the worst mistake of your life."

Eden smiled sadly, kindly, and went in search of Cullen.

# Twelve

Linsey was tired. No. That didn't quite say it. She was exhausted. In the week since she'd spoken with Lincoln, telling him of her decision to leave the lowcountry with Cade, she'd worked day and night, eating little, sleeping less.

The house was cleaner than it had ever been. The barn was spotless and waiting for Jackson's new horses. The garden had been weeded and mulched and pruned to painful perfection.

All that was needed now were responses from the résumés she'd scattered all over the country, and a referral from Davis Cooper. She regretted that it wouldn't be Cooper who would remove Cade's cast. But if the park service came through with a position first, it couldn't be helped. She respected Cooper and trusted that he would recommend the best for Cade.

Cade. Laying her trowel aside and rising from her knees, Linsey moved to the garden gate. Shading her eyes against the afternoon sun, she watched as he played with little energy with Brownie. He was subdued. Not because they were leaving the farm, for she hadn't found the courage to tell him. But he'd always been uniquely intuitive for one so young, and she knew he sensed something was wrong. At first he'd still seen Lincoln in daily visits to Belle Reve. But in this endless week, never at the farm, where Lincoln had once been a part of every day.

Then, abruptly, without offering an explanation, Cade stopped visiting Belle Reve. She'd been fearful at first when he began traveling the trail between the plantation and the farm alone. She'd watched with her heart in her throat as he'd bumped along, somehow managing to peddle his rusty bike despite the encumbering cast. But now that he seemed too worried and too reluctant to leave her, she wished he would venture out again.

"That's odd," an unfamiliar voice growled into the still summer day. "You don't look like a coward, Linsey Stuart."

Startled, she jerked about. An old-fashioned surrey sat only a few yards from the garden fence. An unsmiling Jesse Lee nodded a cool greeting as he held the reins of a handsomely matched pair of horses. But it was the man who sat beside him who captured her attention.

"I beg your pardon." She'd never met Gus Cade, but she would have known him anywhere. Not because he was with Jesse, or even that his right arm hung uselessly by his side, paralyzed by a stroke. Certainly not that he bore any hint of physical resemblance to any of his sons. But there was something, attitude, a manner, something indefinable they shared. Gazes colliding, holding, Linsey asked, "May I help you?"

"It isn't my pardon you should beg. And, yes, by damn, you can help me." Eyes burning with anger seared her. "You can put the starch back in your spine, and while you're at it, quit underestimating the boy."

"Which boy?" Linsey asked sharply, her own anger kindling. "Mine, or yours, Gus Cade."

Gus startled her by chuckling. "Spunk. You've got some after all. Doesn't surprise me, though, you being a self-made woman. From what little Lincoln and his brothers tell me, I believe that's no misnomer—self-made. Against impossible odds, and out of pure cussed determination, I'm told you made yourself into a strong, solid person. It's just too damned bad you don't give your own son the credit of having the same courage. What's worse, you've denied him the choice or the chance to prove what he's made of."

"I have not done that."

"Haven't you?" The horses moved restlessly as if disturbed by some unseen force. Jesse clucked and called, calming them. Beyond gripping the seat with his good hand, Gus Cade hardly noticed. "Have you told the boy you're leaving? Have you told him why? Has it occurred to you that even if he knew the whole story, and what he could face because of it, he might choose to stay?

"Hell, girl. There's no might to it. Cade would choose to stay, and we both know it."

In her heart Linsey believed this angry, old man was right. "He's too young to understand."

"Oh, really?" Gus drawled, graying brows lifted incredulously. "Tell me, sis, just how old were you when you began to understand what you had to do?" He sat ramrod straight, but Linsey saw the effort it took to maintain the posture. "My guess would be when you were the boy's age. Maybe younger. Maybe way back when you were still Hannah Jones. You're a fighter and you're tough. So is Lincoln. I expect young Cade got a goodly share of those genes. So give him a say in this. He deserves it.

"Now—" Gus drew a struggling breath "—that's all I'm going to say on the subject. Dammit, it's all I have the breath to say." His voice softened unexpectedly. "But I would appreciate it if you'd let me take the boy back to

Belle Reve with me for a while. I've missed him these two days.''

If Linsey didn't know Gus Cade personally, she knew him by reputation, and nothing could have surprised her more than the look of loneliness barely hidden in the strong, stubborn face. Suddenly she realized this hard, ornery man, who'd become what he had to become and done whatever he'd had to do to survive, probably understood her better than anyone. Anger fading, she suggested almost kindly, ''Why don't we let your namesake make that decision, Mr. Cade?''

''Would be a start.'' The horses shied in tandem, worried by an invisible irritant. Gus stiffened, glancing at the sky with a questioning look on his face while Jesse calmed the team.

Later, when Cade clambered in the surrey with Brownie, after first covering Linsey's face with kisses, Gus Cade offered a parting bit of advice. ''Watch the weather, girl. There's something strange brewing. Don't know what, but the horses do.''

A tip of hats, a smile from the unusually silent Jesse, and the surrey wheeled about in the clearing. With Cade waving and Brownie barking, it rocked and bounced over the trail returning to Belle Reve.

Linsey was alone, to ponder what Gus Cade had come to say. ''Is he right?'' she asked the land, the sky, the trees, and no one. ''Am I making a choice that should be Cade's?''

Picking up the trowel she began to dig again. ''He's only five, how can he know what he wants?''

In the next thought she admitted that even as young as five she hadn't wanted a name chosen by strange bureaucrats and not her parents. Of course her parents hadn't cared enough for their baby girl to keep her, and certainly not enough to give her a name. So finally after five more years of answering to a name that never seemed to fit, she ceased being the abandoned Hannah Jones and created Linsey Blair, who was determined to conquer the world.

A sympathetic nun, her favorite teacher, her favorite person, had understood and helped. But the actual decision to change her name, and the name of choice, was made by Linsey.

The more she pondered this dilemma, the harder she worked, losing track of time, forgetting Gus Cade's warning. She was only vaguely aware of an eerie stillness, the hollow quiet with random sounds muffled. Mounting heat turned torrid. The only relief from it coming in snatches of cool breezes contrasting with the climbing temperature and bordering on arctic.

If she'd been conscious of anything but her worry over choices and Cade, she would have realized Gus Cade's caution of strange happenings was materializing. But she wasn't aware of sudden changes or of the quickening of the wind. The horse Lincoln was riding was nearly upon her before she knew that on another level of awareness she'd been hearing the powerful drum of its hooves for some time.

"Lincoln." As she stepped past the fence and looked up at him, the sky was a seething mass of drab-gray and dirty-yellow clouds. "What is it?"

"Tornado." The succinct warning was all Linsey needed. Before the word was done, she understood all the danger and reacted. As she reached for Lincoln, their arms meeting, hands clasped at the elbows, he swung her up behind him.

"Cade!" she cried as he spurred Diablo into a run.

"He's safe."

A strong gust whipped the words from his mouth, but Linsey heard. And believed. He wouldn't have said it if it weren't true. "The house."

"No time. The funnel touched down. It's on the ground and coming this way."

Linsey nodded, knowing he couldn't see. Wrapping her arms tighter about his waist she didn't try to speak again as Diablo launched into a dead run. She didn't ask where he was taking her, but as he guided the agile horse over fences and through trees, she understood why he'd come for her on horseback.

The winds grew stronger, the temperature plummeted. As if he had wings and delicate feet, Diablo dodged under-brush and sailed over thickets. The sky was murky, as black as the racing horse. When they entered a clearing Linsey, could barely see and had no idea if it was Cade or Stuart land.

Lincoln was on the ground and lifting her out of the saddle almost before Diablo responded to his tug on the reins. Grasping the reins and hooking his arm through hers, he fought his way forward against a wind that had become ominously steady.

Releasing her briefly, he vaulted into a depression she hadn't seen, and doubted that Lincoln would have if he hadn't known exactly where he was going. As Diablo fol-lowed his master into the swirling leaves that covered the lower ground, Linsey leaped into Lincoln's arms.

"This is the foundation of an old tenant house," he ex-plained with his mouth pressed against her ear. "There's a cellar in the back, in the left corner of what was the kitchen."

Linsey needed no more urging than the slight pressure of his hand at her back. She was running, with Lincoln and Diablo keeping pace, when a tree limb breaking away cracked like a shot. He didn't hesitate or let her falter. They were nearly at the opposite wall when he caught her to him. "Wait here."

First he took a scarf from his pocket and blindfolded the horse, next he stripped off the saddle and laid it a few feet away. While she watched, he brought the great horse down on its side and hobbled it. Without pause, Lincoln went down on hands and knees, sifting through the churning accumulation of years of leaves. Like a miracle in the deepening gloom, she saw the flash of his smile. Then he was straining to open a trap door he'd exposed. Moving as quickly as she could against a wind that had grown sharper and colder, she stood by his side, adding her strength to his. When she despaired that it would ever open, the heavy metal rectangle began to rise inch by eternal inch.

"Not all the way," he warned her with his mouth nearly touching her once more. Even then, and with the wind at his back, she hardly heard. "Can you wedge the saddle into the opening?"

"Yes." She screamed the word, and the wind tossed it back at her. Rather than waste the effort again, touching his arm, she nodded instead.

When it was done, she was shaking and exhausted from the effort, and wondering how much precious time they had used up. Coming to Lincoln's side again, she pressed her lips against his ear. "What about Diablo?"

"I've done all I can for him, Linsey. And we've run out of time. There are steps inside. I'm standing at the head of them." Rain began to fall, plastering their clothing to them in an instant. He heaved the door a notch higher. "Go!" he screamed above the banshee scream of the wind. "Once you're in, brace the saddle at the edge. Don't let it fall, or we might never get out."

As soon as she slipped through the opened wedge, Lincoln crawled in beside her. Linsey had a moment to mutter a prayer of thanks that he was safe, and offered one that no snakes had found their way into the cellar. Then the tornado descended. Like a leviathan gone mad it bore down on the clearing and the bordering forest, shearing and flinging trees like battering rams, destroying everything in its path. For what seemed forever, this most unpredictable beast of nature roared above them. The trapdoor creaked and groaned as if the beast would twist it in half. Instead, as the roar moved up a decibel, threatening eardrums and sanity, it ripped away. Metal screaming like a howling animal, it scraped along the wall of the foundation before going airborne.

Lincoln had been holding her as they lay on damp stone. With their protection gone, he covered her body with his, shielding her, taking the brunt of flying debris. Pressed closely against him, in the absolute darkness the beat of his heart at her back was her anchor. The heart of Lincoln, who would risk his life for her and protect her because he loved her.

It had taken a while, but she'd finally understood that he'd been slow to involve himself in his son's life out of love and fear of hurting him. Now, though she knew it would break his brave heart, Lincoln would let Cade go for the same reason.

Lincoln acted with honor and courage in all that involved Cade. She was the cowardly one.

Caught up in her reflections, deafened by the noise and numbed by battering wind, Linsey was slow to grasp that the forest had grown quiet. In her trance-like state, the monster had come and gone, and they were still alive. "We did it, Lincoln," she cried against the broad hand that shielded her face. "Just like the fire, we survived."

Lincoln didn't respond. He didn't move. "Lincoln!"

Struggling from his protective embrace, Linsey discovered he was unconscious and she was covered in blood. Not her blood, Lincoln's. The blood he'd shared with Cade. Frantic, she knelt over him, searching for injuries. Beyond scratches and a small abrasion, she found only a gaping wound in his scalp. "Help," she muttered. "I have to find help."

Diablo whickered in response to the sound of her voice and tried to get to his feet. Reluctantly leaving Lincoln, but with rising hope, Linsey went to check the horse. After moving branches stripped bare in the storm, she saw the black, gleaming coat was only scratched and nicked. When she took away the bindings and the scarf, the stallion struggled to its feet, then stumbled a step, favoring a foreleg. Mighty Diablo was lame.

Linsey refused to panic, for in panic she would be no help to Lincoln. Struggling to orient herself, she weighed the choice of walking out of the chaos for help, against staying with Lincoln. The decision was made for her when she heard the call of familiar voices. "Here," she answered, and her glad call resounded in desolate stillness. "We're over here."

Soon Adams, Jackson, Jefferson and Cullen were with her, assuring themselves she was unharmed even as they turned their attention to Lincoln. Cullen stayed behind, wrapping Linsey in his Goliath's embrace as if she were as much his charge as Noelle.

"He's okay," Jackson called a second before he touched her shoulder. "Honey," he reassured her as he'd come to do, "he really is okay."

As Cullen released her, she saw that beneath his shock of auburn hair Jackson's wicked grin was not so wicked in an unnaturally pale face.

"Just another knock on the head. For once it's a damned good thing it's so hard, but it's still nothing Cooper can't handle. One thing's for sure—by the time the raging headache stops, he's going to have one hell of a shiner."

Jackson was chattering. He was the most loquacious of the four brothers, but Linsey had never heard him rattle on so nervously. He was trying to reassure her despite his own worry, and she was grateful for the effort. "Thank you, Jackson. I don't know how to begin to repay you."

"There's a way. I doubt I have to spell it out."

"You're asking me to stay?"

Jackson touched her cheek, drying tears she didn't know were streaming down her face. "I'm asking you for my brother's sake to give it a little more time. Test the water. See how things go before you cut and run.''

Linsey bit her lip, her eyes for Lincoln alone as Jefferson and Adams and Cullen helped him from the cellar. ''Is that what you think I'm doing?'' she whispered. ''Running?''

''No,'' Jackson said as quietly. ''I would say it's more a case of a mother being more protective than her son needs.''

Adams came to her. ''The bleeding's stopped, he's conscious and barely lucid. But we can get him to the truck. Jefferson will bring Diablo, and Cooper's meeting us at the farm.''

''The farm?'' Linsey hadn't given it a thought.

''It's still there,'' Adams assured her. ''Most of it. This twister was like a jack-in-the-box, hopping all over. It wiped out your flower garden, took a right turn, skipped over the house taking a stone or two out of the chimney, then obliterated the old shed. What was once your car is scattered over the east pasture.''

''Even so, you were lucky,'' Cullen said as he walked with her on their trek to the truck. ''Lucky Lincoln got to you in time. Lucky he remembered this old foundation and brought you here.''

''Yes,'' Linsey agreed as she walked behind Adams and Jackson with Lincoln braced between them. ''Lucky.''


''Jeepers, doesn't look like a tornado ever came here.''

Cade stood at the edge of the porch, surveying the clearing that no longer looked like a war zone. The one great tree that had been felled by the storm had been cut into logs and stacked away for winter. Thanks to Jefferson the flower garden had been fenced and replanted. Adams's stonemason had made quick work of the chimney repairs, while his cleanup crew cleared debris from the land. The total losses were the shed and Linsey's car. One had disappeared, while the other was declared a total wreck.

In the week since the storm, only Lincoln looked worse as the bruising Jackson predicted spread down his face. But to Linsey, standing in the door watching the two most important people in her life, Lincoln's bruises were marks of valor, and he was gorgeous.

"Cade." Lincoln patted the step where he sat. "Come sit here for a while. I have something to tell you."

Linsey tensed. She and Lincoln had decided it was time to tell Cade the truth. She tried not to be anxious about Cade's reaction and failed miserably.

"Yes, sir." Obediently Cade took the place offered. "I know. Lucky told me."

Lincoln couldn't speak for a moment, and it took every effort not to look back at Linsey. "Lucky told you?" When Cade nodded solemnly, he ventured, "He told you I would have something to tell you?"

"That's part of the secret."

"The secret Lucky said you'd know when to tell and to whom?" Another nod, and this time Lincoln did glance back at Linsey, discovering she was as puzzled as he. "Am I the one who should hear this secret, and is it time?"

Cade took off the Stetson. His chubby fingers stroked the brim as he considered. "I think maybe it is."

"Maybe?" Lincoln asked gently. "Or for sure?"

Cade looked away from the hat. Gray eyes met gray eyes as he searched for something in Lincoln. Finally a quick nod broke the solemn stare. "For sure."

"Do you think your mom should hear this?" Cade answered by sliding closer to Lincoln making room for his mother on the broad wooden steps the boy and the man had repaired together.

"Are you sure you want to do this, Cade?" Linsey asked as she hugged him.

"I been wanting to do it for a long time." His young face wrinkled in a frown, but cleared as he began to speak. "Just before he got so sick, Lucky told me he'd never let me call him dad 'cause he wasn't my dad. He said he'd kinda borrowed me from my real dad, and soon he would be giving me back.''

"Did he tell you who your real dad was?" Lincoln asked, his voice filled with emotion.

"Nope. But he said I would know my real dad when I met him. And even though he didn't know about me, he would know me. But Lucky made me promise I'd be quiet and patient 'cause it would prob'ly take a while for it to get worked out in everbody's mind. He said when it did, my real dad would want me more than anything and love me more than anybody, 'cept Mom.''

Lincoln looked from Cade to Linsey and saw bright tears blinked away before he looked again at the boy. "Do you feel like you've met your real dad?"

A steady, gray regard that seemed far older than Cade's years held Lincoln's. "I think so. I hope so.''

"Do you think I'm your dad?"

Cade caught his lip between his teeth and looked away.

Lincoln saw fear of disappointment in the young serious face. With an arm, he circled small, young shoulders that had born this burden for too long. "Tiger, it's okay to say it, because if what you're thinking and hoping is that I'm your dad—'' tears of pride in a courageous son spilled unashamed down weathered cheeks ''—then you're right.''

Lincoln had no chance to say more as Cade shot up from the step and wrapped little arms tightly around his neck. Lincoln's soft laugh held a bittersweet note as he kissed his son's dark hair. "I'm sorry Lucky borrowed you, but I'm happier he sent you back to me. And he was right, I love you more than anybody, 'cept your mom.''

Linsey was laughing and crying at once. But silently, fearful the slightest sound would end the magic.

"There's one more thing,'' Lincoln said as Cade backed away to look at him. "A choice you have to make. A last name.''

Cade regarded him solemnly now. "Does that means you want us to have the same name?"

"Yes, it does. Like Jesse said about the colt, it's long, long, long past time you know who you are. I want the world to know you're my son. But if you'd rather stay a Stuart, that's okay, too."

"Cade Cade." The boy tried the name. "Sounds kinda funny. But not ha-ha funny."

"How about Leland Stuart Cade," Linsey dared risk a suggestion. "All your names, but rearranged."

Cade considered a minute. "Would I be Leland or Stuart?"

"Why not still Cade?" Linsey asked.

"People might name kids two last names, but they don't get called just by the last."

"Some do." Lincoln intervened. "Davis Cooper, for instance. Only strangers call him Davis. To his friends he's always been Cooper. He always will be."

"Leland Stuart Cade." Cade tried the name again. "Cade. I like it. I like it a lot." He giggled, then sobered as a new thought struck him. "What do I call you?"

"What would you like?"

"I was thinking maybe Dad."

"So was I." Lincoln smiled, liking his new name, too.

"Dad." Cade savored the word. "I never had one before."

"You do now, tiger. For always."

"I guess this means Grampa Gus really is my grampa." A smile grew wider. "Can I go tell him?"

"Sure." Linsey stroked her son's dark hair. "Go tell him. Tell everybody at Belle Reve."

"Ya-hoo!" After scattering kisses over both his mom's and his dad's faces, Cade clumped down the steps, so accustomed to the cast it barely slowed him down.

The bike rattled down the trail and out of sight before

Lincoln turned to Linsey. "Some secret. Lucky was always full of surprises. Looks like he saved the best for last."

"We didn't warn Cade."

"About what people might say?" Lincoln laughed. "Sweetheart, do you really think anything anyone says will truly bother him? I don't, but just in case, we'll teach him to be tolerant of idiots."

"He's so wise for such a little boy. Do you wonder what he'll be like when he's thirty?"

"Who knows?" Lincoln turned her face to him. "Whatever he is, he'll bring strength and the wisdom of Solomon to it."

"He didn't ask questions."

"He will. Dozens, like rapid fire." One kiss brushed over her forehead. "In the meantime, once upon a time in a garden in Belle Terre, I asked a question." A second and a third kiss closed her eyes. "I'd like an answer." His head dipped, his mouth touched hers. "I'd like an answer, *now*."

"You mean will I live with you and be your love?"

"The very same."

Linsey leaned to him, her lips tracing the line of his, her tongue teasing while her fingertips danced a maddening dance over his body. Their caress strayed to his shoulders, then down his arms to twine her fingers through his. A gentle tug had him rising as she murmured, "Cade will visit for a couple of hours. So, why don't I show you?"

"I thought you already had. But I'm game." Drawing a ring from his pocket, Lincoln slipped it on her finger, then kissed her again. "So long as, this time, it's legal."

"Legal or not, I love you, Lincoln. I always have. I always will."

"Till death do us part?"

"No," she whispered against his shoulder as he swept her into his arms to take her to the bedroom where he would make long, leisurely love to her. "For far longer than that." She kissed his throat and laughed when he nearly stumbled. "And, my love willing, many, many more sons."

"How about a daughter or two?"

"Ahh, yes. Cade will be a wonderful older brother."

Lincoln smiled into the tumble of her hair. His little girl lost wasn't lost anymore. And he would give her the family she never had.

"Linsey?" Lincoln said a long while later.

"Yes?"

"There's something I'd like to do."

"Bring Lucky home?"

"How did you know?"

"Because he should be here, with Frannie. With all of us."

"Linsey," Lincoln said, softly. "I love you."

*Linsey, I love you.*

As the words drifted through her mind, Linsey cut one more gardenia. For the second year since Lincoln had brought the plant from the house in Belle Terre to the farm, it bloomed profusely. In summer's heat its perfume filled the air. Bringing the creamy blossom to her face, stroking her cheek with petals wet with morning dew, she remembered another gardenia lying in the tangle of a borrowed gown on a balcony floor. A balcony where Lincoln made love to her and, for the first time, spoke the words.

Words that, with Cade's laughing voice calling out to his dad, were the music of her life. Music, she'd learned, that did not always need a voice.

If she'd known more about love and loving, she would have understood the times Lincoln had said he loved her in silence. "Lincoln," she murmured to the flowers and the sun. "It was always and forever, Lincoln."

Lincoln, hovering, worrying, checking and rechecking her chute before each jump. Suffering a concussion after blocking a sliding boulder meant for her. Teaching her the first of tenderness.

Lincoln, repairing steps, a barn, a farm. Befriending a worshipful little boy, then waiting in a sterile hospital, offering his blood without question.

Lincoln, dancing in the rain. Loving her, making her believe she was beautiful. Letting go because it was what she wanted. Then riding into the furor of a tornado to come for her.

Lincoln, who showed his love in touches and gestures, in simple and wonderful gifts. The best of them, Cade and the baby growing beneath her heart.

With her hand lying against the sweet, tiny bulge of her belly, surrounded in the fragrance of the garden and bittersweet memories, Linsey closed her eyes and lifted her face to the sun. As she listened to the distant peal of Cade's laughter, she knew it would soon be followed by Lincoln's low chuckle.

A sound that always drew her to him, no matter where he was. Linsey was smiling as she bent to take up the basket of flowers that would grace the dinner table tonight when she told him about the baby. "For you, Lincoln," she whispered, "a gift of my love."

He was waiting for her when she reached the creek bank. Waiting to embrace her and hold her, as she knew he would be. And in his silence there was love.

\* \* \* \* \*

*And now turn the page
for a sneak preview of*
*THE TAMING OF JACKSON CADE*

*Book 3 in BJ James's
powerful new miniseries*
MEN OF BELLE TERRE

*On sale in October 2001
from Silhouette Desire*

# One

The grandfather clock in the foyer had boomed the hour five times since Jackson Cade had put Haley in his bed. Four of those times she hadn't heard or stirred. On the fifth, she did.

Slowly, not quite awake, not quite asleep, her lashes fluttered but didn't lift from her cheeks. As the clock fell silent, a frown crossed her face, then was gone.

Six o'clock. She was late. She should be worried, but couldn't muster the energy. Not remembering the night, thinking only of the time, she stirred, beginning a languid stretch, and a sharp pain threatened to slice her in half.

"Ohh." An unfinished breath stopped in her lungs. Lashes that had just begun to rise from her cheeks at last fluttered down in an effort to seal away a world too bright and agony too sharp. She couldn't breathe, she couldn't move, as muscles across her back and midriff held her in paralytic misery.

Denying the pain, she tried to move again, and her teeth

clenched a second too late to bite back a groan. A sound that brought with it the fleeting stroke of a hand across her brow. One offering comfort, but she didn't understand.

"No," she whispered hoarsely and turned away.

"Shhh. Everything's all right, thanks to you. You're all right," a voice assured.

*Thanks to you. Thanks to you.* She'd heard the routine before, trying to soothe what couldn't be soothed, undo what couldn't be undone, by planting a lie. God help her, she'd heard it all before and didn't want to hear it again. Keeping her eyes closed tightly, weary of an old struggle, she whispered, "Don't."

Haley was too tired. The words hurt too much. "Just don't." In the darkness of her world, she shuddered as the bed dipped beneath his weight. "Go away, Todd. Leave me alone."

"Shhh, shhh. Easy." A deep voice, not the obsequious wheedle she expected. "I'm not Todd, Duchess. I don't think I'd like to be. But I won't touch you if you don't want me to."

The voice she'd heard soothing a frightened, crazed horse. Soothing her as gently.

"Jackson?" Gold-tipped lashes lifted. As she risked the turn to face him, eyes once as brilliant as a bluebird's wing were shadowed with more than physical hurt. Her gaze cleared, settling on his frowning features. As she remembered the night and the clock, deducing where she was, she checked a sharply drawn breath. Agony like the first crushed her ribs and spine in its vice.

Jackson watched her pallor grow more ghostly, and under his breath he cursed a man called Todd for sins he couldn't name, and himself for his own folly. "You're safe, Haley. And, because of you, so is Dancer."

"Dancer." The name fell from stiff lips as she remembered the stallion, suffering the throes of madness. "He's alive?"

"Thanks to you. He'll need some time to recover, but eventually he should be good as new."

"How? When?" Haley was discovering there was a gap in her memory. The last she remembered was taking her hand from Jackson's and slipping into Dancer's stall.

"You guessed right on the cause of his symptoms. He was on the edge of another siege when you got the needle in him. Whether it was the needle, the injection, or the cycle of fits, Dancer crushed you against the stall wall."

To Jackson's disgust, by the time he'd recognized Haley's intent, it was too late. Dancer had knocked her aside as if she weighed nothing at all. She'd crumpled into a heap nearly beneath the horse's flying hooves before Jackson could get to her. The time it took to tear open the stall door to shield her was the longest of his life.

"You have a bad bruise." Because he'd let her go. "And you'll be sore a while." His fault, for calling her at all. "But Coop says you'll be right as rain in a week or so."

"Coop? Cooper." She focused on the name, questioning and interpreting all at once. She heard nothing else Jackson said once she knew he was speaking of the dashing Davis Cooper, Belle Terre's physician and bachelor extraordinaire. Her escort for the concert. A friend who, over dinner, subtly made her aware that he'd like more than friendship from her.

Abruptly, in her rush to answer the call to River Trace, she'd left him with barely an explanation or a backward glance. Not the way to treat a kind and gallant man. A would-be lover.

Haley struggled to sit up, unaware that in her cautious efforts the broad shoulder of the shirt she wore slipped down her arm. "I should have called him. I should explain." Not sure what Davis Cooper should know, or how she could begin to explain what she didn't understand herself, she abandoned the muddled thought. "I need to apologize."

"For what, Duchess?" Jackson zeroed in on the little of the ramble he could decipher. "For doing your job? And doing it too zealously and too well?"

An understatement and a far cry from what he'd expected of her. No matter that she was Lincoln's associate, or that his brother would not choose a partner with lesser standards than he expected of himself, in his own stubborn mind-set Jackson knew he'd been unreasonable, believing only the worst of her.

"How I do my job isn't the point."

"Isn't it?" A questioning eyebrow inched up. A typical Jackson Cade reaction, usually accompanied by a teasing smile. But at the moment, with his conscience in turmoil, the typical Jackson Cade was having trouble finding anything to smile about. "Do you really believe that?"

"Of course I do. My work, underdone or excessive, isn't the point of the apology. Common courtesy is. Cooper behaved like a gentleman, the least I can be in return is considerate."

*Touché,* Jackson thought, though he knew there was no intended barb in the remark. He suspected she'd tolerantly filed away the memory of his behavior in the barn as one more Cade foible. If she remembered at all. Suddenly Jackson wasn't sure he liked being dismissed so easily. Even at his insufferable best.

Indifference. The passiveness of indifference was the last thing he expected from Haley Garrett. As she lay in his bed with his shirt refusing to stay properly in place, he had no idea what he wanted. Or didn't want…except indifference.